I0778003

Aggie's War

Willow River Press is an imprint of Between the Lines Publishing. The Willow River Press name and logo are trademarks of Between the Lines Publishing.

Between the Lines Publishing
1769 Lexington Ave N, Ste 286
Roseville MN 55113
btwnthelines.com

First Published: June 2025

ISBN: (Paperback) 978-1-965059-50-0

ISBN: (eBook) 978-1-965059-51-7

Aggie's
War

Bonnie Meekums

"This reads like an authentic diary which draws you in to a very personal and vivid world—a uniquely personal story."

- June Craven, Writer, Quaker, and Disability Activist.

"This is the second book I've read and enjoyed by the author. The diary format makes the story more personal and intimate. I was proud of Aggie for all she gave up but also achieved."

- Tina Probets, Librarian

In memory of Mum, who survived the war and who showed me what a strong woman looks like, and to all those who strive for equality and peace.

15th September 1940

Mum and Dad are dead.

No-one understands how it feels to have lost first, my birth mother when I was so young, now them. My Stan does his best. It's my fault. I've never really confided in him. So, I'm writing down the chatter inside my head. It's got to be better than listening to the space between silence and bombs.

I found this old writing book up in the loft. After the hit that took Mum and Dad, I got it into my head that I'd better take a look up there, just in case we get bombed out. As I stroked the dust of years off its soft leather cover, I could see the pride on Dad's face when he handed it to me. It was the first Christmas after our Adam was born. I must have put it up there for safe keeping—or to hide away my guilt at not using it.

So, here I am at the living room table, one hand curled round my scrawl. I've pushed back the chenille tablecloth so as to have a hard surface under me, and so as not to spill the ink on anywhere that matters. The kids are tucked up in the Anderson shelter in the back garden, I've washed up, and the sirens haven't gone yet. I've told Stan I'm writing my sister-in-law a letter, so I'd better do that too, while I'm at it. I've got a couple of sheets of writing paper at the ready, just in case he looks up. I don't want him seeing this. He'll think I've gone soft in the head. He's not bothered what I'm doing, if truth be told—he's too caught up in the home service. He's sitting on one of the hard chairs, his ear glued to the wireless, shoulders hunched over and a woodbine in his hand, the ash hanging long. Occasionally, he takes a puff and then smoothes his thick wavy hair back from his forehead. One knee bobs up and down, as if he were cold but I know he isn't. He has that look in his eyes that tells me his worries aren't to be shared with me. It's men's business.

We never believed it would start, not when Mr. Chamberlain came back with his bit of paper. But then before we knew it, we were at war. We all had the jitters. The sirens went, but nothing happened. After Chamberlain went off with his tail between his legs last year, Churchill told us it would be blood, sweat and tears, putting the fear of God in us. Still nothing happened. We all breathed again, absorbing ID cards and ration books into our workaday lives. Until, that is, just over a week ago—September 7th—the first night of what they're calling the London Blitz. That was the night Jerry took my Mum and Dad from me.

They've all been to offer their condolences, those that knew them, which of course is everyone in the street, the vicar and most of the congregation, plus the people I see at the Co-op and corner shop. I've come to dread seeing people. I've not dared step outside to scrub my steps, not that I'm ungrateful. Some have just knocked on the door, on spec you might say, and said they're sorry to hear, and if there's anything they can do, you know. One or two brought a little something, like a card made by one of their kids, or a few flowers from the garden. I force a smile, and thank them for their kindness, but I'm glad to shut the door. I don't want them to see how tiny I feel inside. I'm collapsing in on myself. I can smell my own fear. I keep telling myself: Aggie, stop shaking like a little kid. You're a grown woman. A mother of four.

16th September 1940

I've never told anyone my secret. Not even Stan. I've told him bits—enough to keep him happy, like the fact that I had a mama before I came to live with Mum and Dad—but I've never told him the whole truth. He's a man of few words. Not like me. Words spill out of me like kids from the playground at the end of the school day. But not about that. There are some beans that are best not spilled.

There's something else I don't talk about, and all. If I did, they'd say I was off my rocker and send me packing to Bexley, so I keep it tucked away, like the best china. I sometimes go and visit Mama—the woman who brought me into this world. I call it going on my travels. It started soon after I came to London. After that first, long journey that tore me from all I loved. Some might call it dreaming, that is if they didn't say I'm barking, but to me it's as real as this pen in my hand. Last night, as I shut my eyes for sleep, I could feel myself being pulled down through the bed. It usually starts like that—a feeling of being pulled—and then I know I'm going. I mostly go to the same place: the big old house with its wide staircase for Sir and Ma'am, where we lived until I was four. It gives me such a feeling of peace, sitting beside her as she works.

It's funny how I've never told anyone, but I'm telling you, a complete stranger—if anyone ever finds this. But then, I won't ever meet you, will I? If this is ever found, it will mean I've popped my clogs.

It's the coming back after going on my travels that makes me feel sad, because Mama isn't here. It wasn't so bad when I had Mum and Dad living down the road. But there's just a pile of rubble there now, where once there was a home full of life and comings and goings. Death hangs over it like a smog on the Thames.

But I've got my Stan. He makes me feel safe, or a bit less scared at any rate. He takes care of all the decisions. I don't have to worry about a thing. As long as there's food on the table, the house is clean, and the kids are well cared for, he's as happy as Larry. And on his one day off, we're together as a family. He's not one to go down the pub and spend all his earnings, then come home and beat his wife and kids. Not like poor Madge up the road. No. On Fridays, pay day, first thing he does when he comes through that door is he puts my housekeeping in my hand. I don't have to deal with the bills or anything. He takes care of all that. I wouldn't know where to start.

But I didn't know if I was coming or going last night, watching him with that wireless.

17th September 1940

This can't be happening. It's just about the worst timing ever. Not only did Jerry take my Mum and Dad with their deadly fireworks. Now they want to take my old man, too. Stan got his call-up papers yesterday, after I'd finished writing in this thing. He's off to war. Says he's always fancied going to sea. To hear him, you'd think it was a fancy party he was going to, not a blood bath. I've seen enough round here, especially in the past week, since the bombing started. Severed limbs, thinking I could see bits of Mum and Dad scattered halfway across the street. Even before that, women weeping. Telegrams. Those dreaded telegrams.

Last night, I got the kids in their pyjamas and laid the mattresses out as usual—I'd aired them as best I could during the day, but they were still a bit damp. This morning, I woke to hear my youngest, Stephen, coughing. It sounds really bad, like the cough Auntie Barbara's little boy, Colin, used to have. Everyone used to tell me I had to be kind to him, because he was delicate. I'm not sure what happened to him— they moved away when I was about six—but the sound of that cough stayed with me. And last night, the sound of Stephen coughing all night made my insides feel like a jumper that's shrunk in the wash. But what could I do? We're all crowded in there together—me, Stan, Adam, Henry, David and little Stephen. Knowing I have to keep going all day come what may, I rolled over and tried to get some shuteye, but I kept waking, terrified. Anyroad, I must have dropped off because this morning I woke about seven, and we were all drenched. The ruddy shelter had let the rain in. Stan has decided. Tonight, we're taking our chances with the bombs. I'm going to put the old oak table up against a load bearing wall in the living room, and all the mattresses under that. I'll sleep on the outside with Stan. God help us.

But there's another thing. Something I've not mentioned to anyone yet, but in for a penny, in for a pound. Here I am again, with my monthlies having done a runner, leaving behind a calling card that will only grow into more trouble. And I feel as sick as if I had been at the medicinal brandy and drunk the lot. In fact, I just vomited in the middle of writing the bit about the Anderson shelter. It must have been that time when we were using the French letter, and he fell asleep with it still inside me. His brother Tom had persuaded him to come for a pint to wish him luck, because he—Tom, that is—had been called up. I knew what he was going to want when he came in drunk, and sure enough I had to sort him out afterwards.

I won't bother going to the doctor. We haven't got the money anyway. I'll just carry on. There's nothing to be done about it. Maybe shifting the table will bring on a bleed, if I'm lucky. But my babies tend to be plucky little so-and-sos, hanging onto my insides for all they're worth. I daresay there'll be another mouth to feed in about seven months or so. But whether to tell Stan or not, is the question? Will it give him something to stay alive for, or will it mean he takes his eye off the ball?

I must make sure he takes a photo of us on our wedding day with him, to keep in his top pocket. Oh, that was a day, that was. Luckily, my mum is—was, God rest her poor soul—a good seamstress. She ran up a dress for me from some old scraps she got at a jumble sale. Good as new. And she found a lovely headdress, orange blossom and still in good nick. Somebody else's heartache, but I tried to put that out of my mind. It's in mothballs now, in the drawer at the bottom of our wardrobe. I check on it every spring, just to make sure it's still all there.

I'm in a right mood today. It's been raining cats and dogs, and so the kids have all been under my feet. Every time I turn round, one of them seems to be wanting something.

"Mum, when's tea?" (Henry and David, in unison)

"Mummy! Where Teddy?" (Stephen, in tears, of course, reverting to baby talk as he always does when he's upset).

I've had no patience with them.

"Tea'll be ready when it's ready. Now, go away and leave me alone!"

"I don't know where your rotten teddy is, and I don't care! Now stop your crying, or I'll give you something to cry about! Adam! Help your little brother find his teddy, for God's sake, before I swing for him!"

I suppose some might say I've got every right to be out of sorts, what with losing Mum and Dad, bombs falling all round us every night, putting kids to bed in a leaky Anderson shelter, my old man getting his call up papers, and now me being up the duff. I don't know if I'm Arthur or Martha. It's enough to make anyone get out of bed the wrong side — if, that is, they've got a proper bed to get out of.

I don't know how I'm going to cope without my Stan. I always rely on him to be there, to know what to do. I'm shaking. Like I was the day they peeled my fingers away from Mama.

19th September 1940

Last night, after laying all the kids' clothes out for the morning, I pretty well fell into our bed on the floor. This is what happened next.

It's as if someone's got their arms round me from underneath, pulling me down with a force I can do nothing about. As my eyes close, I feel myself falling, but I'm not scared. I've felt this many times before, and it makes me happy, because I know where I'm going.

I come to, and it's daylight. I'm sitting by Mama. She looks just as young and beautiful as the day they took me from her, her dark curls resting on her shoulders, neat as ever, and that lovely mole on her left cheek that she used to touch and call her beauty spot. As she sweeps the grate in the parlour of the big house, she sings a little song to herself, in our language, though I can't catch the words, no matter how hard I strain my ears. If only I could sing along with her.

I sit for some time, just watching and listening, and eventually she sits back on her heels and turns to me, smiling. I feel all warm and glowing inside, my eyes locked onto her face, wishing this moment to last forever.

"Hello, love," she says, like she's just noticed I've popped in to see what she's doing.

I long to reach out and touch her soft, warm skin, but I feel myself hurtling through space. I try to call out to her, but the words get caught in my throat like birds in a cage. I land with a thump, Stan snoring beside me. I turn my head the other way and curl up in a little ball, to suffocate my tears.

22ⁿᵈ September 1940

I've decided I can't keep writing every day, so I'll just write when I have something to say.

I don't only go travelling when I'm asleep, by the way. It can happen when I'm awake, sometimes. On my early visits to Mama, as a little girl, I listened for her singing. Sometimes, in those days, I sang along. But if I slipped away during our daytime and forgot myself and sang out loud, Mummy would bring me back with a thud to England.

"What are you singing, you silly little thing? No one can understand you. Either sing in English, or hold your tongue, otherwise people will think you're wrong in the head."

In time, I learned to do it differently. I found if I sang inside my head and didn't open my eyes, I could also block my ears to Mummy's high-pitched sing-song voice. I say sing-song, but it wasn't like my Mama's song, which was low and rhythmic and called me. It still does. Mummy's sing-song did not call me to sing along. It jarred my body like the sounds of the sirens do now.

Other times, as I ran through the woods behind our house and up into the park with my mates, I felt almost happy. I could walk outside the gate and along the back of the terrace and stand there outside one garden where two brothers lived. One of them had had the polio, and he wore calipers, so he was a bit slow, but his little brother was fast like the wind. I used to stand there and call: "A-lan! Matthew!" And pretty soon they'd be charging out their back door, slinging scarves round their necks as they sped up the path as best they could, flinging open their gate to shouts from their mother to remember to shut it. The gate always swung casually back and fro, waiting for their return.

29th September 1940

I haven't had the energy to write for a while. It's hard, with four boys aged five, six, nine and ten. What with all the usual stuff, the extra work entailed with there being a war on, and the vomiting, I haven't had a chance to draw breath.

Since the Blitz started, sleep is a puppy that just won't come to heel. It's not just the noise and the house shaking. It's more the thought that this one could have my name on it. My heart races as soon as night falls, and I break out in a cold sweat. I don't let on to the kids of course. They think it's all a bit exciting, all these bangs and the sky lighting up, like November the fifth every night. I go along with it, paste a cheery smile on my face as I get them ready for bed. I pull the flannel out with the same stern face as always, scrubbing behind their ears to the usual protests. Each night, in fitful sleep, I catch a train or a boat or both. I trudge through snow and skin splitting deserts, looking for scattered parts of my parents, to bring them home. It always ends the same way. I'm in a fast-flowing river, clinging to something solid, but my fingers aren't strong enough and I feel myself slipping away. Then I wake, my nightie damp and a hammering in my ears.

Now, what little security I had is shattered. No more warm strong chests. No more arms around me. For today, Stan—my rock—left on a train. Of course, they don't want people to know where they're sending their men. I wish I could have stood and watched him embark on his ship.

Last night, as he knelt to say prayers with the boys, their hands clasped to their chests like little angels, I thought he might tell them. But all he did was kiss their foreheads in turn, murmuring his usual "Night-

night, God bless, sleep well, sweet dreams, and…"—I could hear his throat catch as he completed his recital with—"…I'll see you in the morning."

I decided not to tell him just yet, about me having a bun in the oven, which only makes me feel more alone. I—alone—am trying to keep four children and an unborn one safe. It's just me and the kids, and vomiting, and a leaky Anderson shelter, and an oak table against a wall that wouldn't save anyone from a direct hit. My only consolation is there are women all around me, going through similar problems. I wish I could really *feel* that we are all in this together—me and my neighbours, increasingly just women and children now. I had a little cry on Mavis' shoulder—she was saying goodbye to her Fred at the same time—even though I know she's the vicious cow who spread rumours about my Stan playing away.

Anyhow, the men were all smiles and high jinks, off to be lads together, but my stomach turned somersaults as I held on tight to Stephen's hand on one side, and David's on the other, both looking bewildered and shaking from their heels to their heads. Adam took care of Henry, bless him. He's a good lad, is Adam. Even though his dad had said nothing to him until it was time for us to walk across the common, it was as if he'd known for some time. Of course, Stephen was all wriggles and wanting to let go of my hand, and David wanted to run to his daddy. He couldn't see why he wasn't allowed to have a ride on the train, too. I shouted at them to behave, but they wouldn't stand still. I wished I'd had a hand free to wave. But I didn't. And my bloody eyes. I missed my last glimpse of him, because they misted up like a beer glass on a winter's night. After the train had left and I was sure the boys wouldn't fidget anymore, I turned round and poured my guts on the tracks, like emptying soup from a pan.

Now he's gone, I don't know what I'm going to do with myself. Of course, there's still the same old housework and cooking and lugging the shopping and putting the hankies on to boil and washing and ironing and polishing the top step, sweeping and scrubbing the other steps. But who am I going to talk to in the evenings and share a cup of tea with, as I listen to the wireless and they try to convince us all we've had a good day fighting Jerry? They must think we're all bloody stupid. Mind you, some are. Some actually believe the rubbish they hear. But all I see is the ruins, and the smouldering buildings, and the women weeping, and the growing numbers of deaths reported in the Kentish Independent. I'm not daft. This is no glorious war.

There was another war, the day I arrived in England. The so-called Great War started that day. August 4, 1914. That was supposed to be the war to end all wars. And here I am again, a world war raging, and me feeling just as desperately alone as I did then. Just as at sea.

There were other times, back then, when the pain of not being with Mama got dark as a new moon at midnight. Then, it seemed impossible to zip over to the other side of the world and get close to her. I realised whenever I did visit her, there was one thing missing. I could never actually snuggle up to her. Never feel her breath, or her hand idly fiddling with my hair. She was never able to kiss me. Except when I was asleep. Then, it was so real I could taste it. Until I woke up.

30th September 1940

Stan's departure has left me thinking about things I'd rather not remember. And not just about the rumours Mavis spread.

God alone knows how I managed to go from the little girl who always hid behind her mum to being a wife and mother myself. I didn't even know where babies came from when I met Stan. He took me up the hill for a walk the day after he proposed. There was a bitter wind, despite it being summer. I had my shawl round my shoulders, but it didn't stop the cold poking its nasty long fingers under my clothes. I might as well have been naked. When he laid me down on the grass, I couldn't stop shivering, especially when he reached up under my skirt and pulled my drawers down. I pinched my eyes together, willing myself to disappear. You might ask why I didn't stop him, but you see, I was brought up not to complain or make a fuss. I just hoped whatever he was doing would soon be over. Then we could pretend it never happened.

It was like a knife slicing into me. There was a lot of huffing and puffing, and he went proper red. But it only lasted a short while. He fumbled about trying to pull my knickers up, but then gave up. He stood and looked away so I did it myself, wishing I could just sink into the earth. I looked at his back. Was this what men did to you? I had no one to ask, so I thought I'd better just accept it. I was his now.

I held my shawl tight over my head and shoulders as we walked back down the hill, but he grabbed one of my hands, squeezing it so tight my knuckles rubbed against each other, and I nearly cried out. As we parted, he kissed me on the lips, dripping saliva into my mouth. I could smell and taste the beer he'd drunk before he called for me. And then, as if he'd never hurt me, he stroked my cheek and spoke with a tenderness I've not heard from him since, matched by a look in his eyes that under any other circumstances would melt even the hardest of hearts:

"Aggie, my love. We'll be alright on our wedding night." He gave me a peck on the cheek. "Until tomorrow."

He didn't do it again, until we were married. That time, it didn't hurt nearly as much. We intended to wait a full year before being wed, but when Mum realised I'd missed three monthlies, just as my upset tummy was calming down, she asked if Stan had "done it" to me. I didn't know what she meant, so I asked her. She looked red and spat as she explained:

"Did he lie you down and put his thing inside you?"

I must have looked as dumb as Daft Doris, that girl down the street who's never learned to read and write. Mum's face was as near to exploding as I've ever seen anyone's.

"Down below!"

My face probably went the colour of the blood I was no longer getting, because she took it as a yes. We met the vicar the next day and were married within the month, on the day I turned twenty-one—November 20, 1930. Nearly eleven years ago.

Anyway. That's what's been coming back to me, now that he's gone away.

1ˢᵗ October 1940

I wouldn't want anyone reading what I wrote yesterday to think I'm not happily married. That was a long time ago, and to be honest, I'd put it all to the back of my mind. I've no idea why it should bite me on the bum now. Probably just feeling a bit nervy, what with the bombs, and being pregnant, and my old man being away God knows where, facing God knows what.

Adam has gone silent, Henry's been picking on David, who of course ends up in tears and hiding in my apron, while Stephen just keeps crying for his daddy. Just when you're at your lowest, if you're a mum you can't spend long feeling sorry for yourself. I ended up shouting at the lot of them to leave me alone for five minutes today, promising to give them all a clip round the ear if they didn't.

5ᵗʰ *October 1940*

I've been exhausted since Stan left. You'd think life would get easier without a man to look after, but then I've been like a cat on hot bricks.

I worry about Adam. Being the oldest, he takes so much on his little shoulders. When we had him, we weren't really ready to be parents. We'd hardly got used to being a married couple, to be fair. Five months was all we had before he burst into our world, ten and a half years ago. Still, I was over the moon, and of course Stan was too, to have a son. I think a man needs a son. I was that happy I didn't stop to ask myself what others would think of us. I was a married woman. Respectable. And a mother. Finally, I had someone that no one was ever going to take away from me. Of course, we told everyone he'd come early and waited a bit before we allowed anyone to see him, but I could feel the eyes on me when I pushed his pram out for the first time. Like blowtorches on my back.

It was hard, being a first-time Mum, trying to get used to being a wife. I hadn't got a clue how to look after a baby. Mum wasn't much use, even though she'd had a boy herself. It's like she didn't feel confident around me, all of a sudden. So, I had no help, really. No guidance about burping, or what to do when they won't stop screaming, or how often to change the nappy, or feeding—what to do when you're so sore all you can do is tense up and cry. He took a long while to get the hang of feeding. He got so scrawny I feared he might die. I used to sit and stare into space. More often than not, I'd pick him up and find he'd been lying in his mess so long he'd got a fiery rash.

Eventually I managed to pull myself together and do what was right, but then he seemed to go into his shell. No amount of coaxing would draw him out. As soon as he could hold a spoon he wanted to feed himself. He was walking by ten months. Dressing himself, buttons and all, at three.

Of course, by the time Henry came along I'd got the hang of being a Mum. I wasn't so miserable about it. Plus, what with them being a year and a bit apart, I wasn't so sore feeding him. I fell in love with his blond curls. Also, when I was pregnant the second time, once the sickness wore off, I started enjoying the other thing. The thing that makes the little blighters in the first place. What's more, Stan quite enjoyed me enjoying it, which surprised me. I got quite bold, even showing him where to touch me. It fair caught my breath, when he got the hang of it.

I went off it again after we had Henry, with two little ones to look after, so I had a bit of a break from being pregnant. But then I overheard Mavis in the corner shop, telling her friend she'd seen Stan outside the Mitre with some floozy. So, I forced myself to get interested again. With the result that along came David on June 12, 1934, named after my brother. Stephen followed hot foot the next year.

After Stephen, we discussed whether or not to have another. I was still worried he'd go off with some bit of fluff if I didn't play ball, but then Stan explained we could use this thing called a French letter so we could still do the deed but not have the consequences. It seemed too good to be true! Actually, I enjoyed it more once I knew I couldn't get pregnant. But that didn't work for long, did it?

I'll be in bed as soon as I've finished the washing up. The tiredness you get in early pregnancy always knocks me for six. I could sleep on a clothesline.

I often wonder how my Mama is doing, if she's alive. Am I making it all up, when I go to see her? Do I have any brothers and sisters there? Are any of them fighting? I don't seem to be hopping over there as often as I used to, swapping time and place in my upside-down world. Too busy chasing Londoners across the world, or rather bits of them. Maybe I need to concentrate harder. Maybe it will happen when the time's right.

6th October 1940

Well, it's happened. Just not in the way I wanted.

I'm sitting in my chair; the kids are in bed; and I'm darning one of Adam's socks on the Bakelite mushroom Mum gave me last Christmas, little salty droplets gathering in my eyes and making it hard to see. The wireless is chattering away. My ears prick up at a news item about the land of my birth. There's a battalion made up of our people. A man with a plum in his mouth is interviewing some of the soldiers. I chuckle, certain he won't understand them. They're deliberately (I suspect) talking in as heavy an accent as they can muster.

I feel myself shrinking. It's not the feeling of falling I'm used to, and I panic. I don't want this. I want to see Mama. But I can't stop it. Before I know it, I'm smaller than the head of the needle I was holding, just seconds ago. Then, the sucking feeling starts, but not downwards. I'm being sucked into the wireless, through the tiny holes moulded into the casing.

When I emerge on the other side, I can hear the soldier like I'm standing next to him. I feel I'm home. That voice—so strong and familiar, even after all these years. I can see him, too—a warrior, thick-set, swirling tattoos on his face. He looks handsome. I feel drawn to him, a solid feeling in my chest telling me he is my people. My family. We share a genealogy. I remember seeing marks like those when I was little, before I was taken. When Mama had a day off, we sometimes travelled many miles to see family, or they would come to us. Some of the warriors looked like him. If I wanted to, I could reach out and touch his face, tracing the lines inked into his skin. But I stand, silent and still. He speaks of his pride at being able to fight for his country. He never mentions Britain, the country that requires his allegiance despite the treaty. Just "his" country, which I know means the land of our ancestors.

I stand there a good half-hour, a kind of birth cord linking my heart to his. I know he feels it too. It's so strong. It vibrates, pulsating along with the unseen moon. My fear has completely gone. I can't help feeling I'm meant to be here, to give him strength which I now have in buckets. It occurs to me, as if this is an everyday thought, that it's the unborn child giving me some kind of feminine power, as I pour all the colours of the rainbow into him.

And then, I feel myself being sucked back through the wireless, despite kicking and protesting, across to the other side. My body hurts like nothing on earth. I feel bruised and battered and drained when I once again find myself full-size, back in my chair, my sewing discarded on the floor. The wireless is silent.

12th *October 1940*

The vomiting has got even worse. I'd better not be carrying twins. Mind you, I'm sure the poor state of my nerves isn't helping. I'll wait until I'm better before I tell Stan I'm expecting.

I was stood talking to Mrs. Mitchell down the road—she insists on being called Mrs. Mitchell even though I know her Christian name is Iris—and she was going on about the young of today, and how they should all have volunteered by now, and how we'll win this war with Churchill at the helm. And I just leaned over and vomited right beside her. I think a bit splashed onto her rather nice brocade shoes. She pulled her handbag under her bosom, poked her nose in the air and said, "Well!" as if no one ever threw up before when they're up the duff. Stuck up old cow. I bumped into my old china Shirley after that and told her. We had a giggle. I've known Shirley since we were kids. She was the first girl in my primary school to befriend me, despite me not having a tongue in my head when I first arrived. She used to take hold of my arm and lead me to places where I was meant to be. She also taught me cat's cradle and skipping games like the one where you have two ropes going at once, and that game where you use your fingers to make a church, a steeple and then the people. She had an old tennis ball and we found another in the woods, so we could play two balls in her backyard up against the kitchen wall. We'd sing rhymes as we played, like, "My father was a captain on the Lusitania," except we said, "Luisadia." I wish we still played, as wives and mothers. When children play, no one cares if you look different, or you don't speak the same language. I still had lots of the old words in my head in those days. English words sat crammed in my mouth, imposters to be spat out, or swallowed out of sight. Play seems to create a world of its own. It's the glue that makes it possible to rub along together. We need more of that. Like when during the Great War, the soldiers from both sides played football in No Man's Land. I'd love to join a women's football team, even though I've never been to a match. It would make a change from polishing and digging in rubble. I've heard some of the munitions factories have women's teams.

The kids have all got colds. No surprise there. The weather's getting chillier now, and I can't afford to heat their bedrooms. I worry about the little one, Stephen. He seems to have a weak chest, poor love. It's hard, not having Stan around. Not that he ever did much to help—I just felt safer with him here, and he made the kids feel safe, too. Mind you, the women in the neighbourhood do all seem to be pulling together. Even the ones that usually spend their time tittle-tattling about everyone else seem to have realised that's a lonely place to be. I got a smile off old Ma West the other day. She nodded her head at me and said, "morning," as if she's never been nasty to me in her life. Funny, that. I wonder whether she'll go back to her old ways, talking about people behind their backs, once the war's over.

Somebody told me, and I've no idea how true this is, that the Jews in Germany are having to wear stars to identify themselves. It seems Mr. Hitler doesn't go a bundle on Jews. I just hope he doesn't invade us, like he did Poland. He's already got onto the continent, and I heard on the news he's even got as far as the Channel Islands. It's not a good time to be at sea, but Stan was adamant that's what he wanted. I lie awake at night, worrying. My poor thinking cap does overtime. I try to pull it off, but it won't budge. Sometimes, I think about what I'd do if our house got hit. How I'd reach out for the kids and hold on for dear life. If we die, we die together. I can't bear to think of one of them poor little mites being without his mummy, facing death alone.

28th October 1940

Time to make my Christmas pudding and Christmas cake. Mrs. Featherstone down the road told me how to do it, what with the rationing and food shortages. I've been saving some of my rations week by week so I have what I need. It's easy enough to make the breadcrumbs since I started baking my own bread, and the big tip Mrs. Featherstone gave me was to use a bit of white vinegar instead of the lemons and oranges, because of course they're hard to come by. So, I did, and Bob's your uncle! It works just as well. Eggs are also scarce, but not yet rationed. No doubt that'll come. I've learned to store them the pointy side down in a rack that's sat in a pail of waterglass to keep them fresh. And here's the genius bit—four ounces of grated carrot to keep the cake moist (plus a splash of milk) because you only use four ounces of butter and the same of sultanas to a pound of whole-wheat flour and another pound of breadcrumbs. I tossed in as much dried fruit as I could find—prunes, dates, currants—about six ounces in all. Of course, I had to pick it all over, take out the stones and stalks. I put a bit of Tate and Lyle golden syrup in, for the sugar. I had the pudding steaming away all day yesterday, with the usual silver coin in it wrapped up in greaseproof paper. Needless to say, I had to let the kids lick the mixture, it being a Sunday and all.

After getting that simmering, I started on the cake. A bit of a cheat because the mixture's very similar. It was a struggle to find the ingredients for both, but I like to get them out the way at this time of year, then feed each regularly, with a spot of brandy. When I feed them, I make several holes with a knitting needle, then pour carefully. You only need a little brandy each time, but it adds a lovely flavour and preserves it.

By the time I'd finished all this baking my insides felt really keen to get to know the toilet bowl again.

24

10th November 1940

Today I was feeling a bit better, despite the temperature dropping. Bonfire night came and went, but there was no fire, no fireworks—other than those deadly ones. I know I haven't written in a while. I do hope you don't think I'm abandoning you, dear reader from the rubble—though, of course, I'm making you up! It helps me to imagine I'm writing to a real person, someone who, despite not knowing me, cares whether or not I feel sick, whether I survive these bombs or am blown to smithereens.

The cold gets under your clothes and into your bones, filling every crevice like water seeping between rocks. We get bombs every night, soon as it turns dark. It's being so close to Woolwich Arsenal, you see. That's what they're after, and they don't care that there are women and children and old people in the way. They want to cause maximum damage. No doubt we're doing the same over there, but then we're the goodies, aren't we?

Today I volunteered to help clear rubble while the kids were at school. With no man to keep the house spick and span for, I might as well be out of the house making myself useful. I got chatting to a slightly older woman. I reckon she's about forty—streak of grey hair under her hat, like chalk on a blackboard.

"Hello," she says, holding a grubby hand out towards me. I figure mine's just as dirty, so I offer it back. We tend to keep our gloves on while we work the rubble over, in the vain hope we might be able to prevent that feeling that our fingers are dropping off. We start off feeling the warmth from our woollen gloves, but then the cold barges in and the pain gnaws away at you. After a while, your fingers go numb which makes it difficult to feel, so you go home with cuts and bruises you never knew you had. The worst pain is when you begin to thaw out and the blood comes back.

"Name's Hilda. What's yours?" She's already back to lugging large bits of rubble and placing them into the designated area.

"Aggie," I say. I can't help smiling. This is the first time I've done more than grunt to anyone, clearing rubble.

Then we both hear it. I stop working, wishing it was the wireless and I could turn up the volume or tune in the station. There it is again. So quiet I would think I'd imagined it if Hilda hadn't stopped too, cocking her head.

We both start working furiously. She scrapes away and hands me stuff to put on the pile, then without discussing it, we swap over. It's my hand that uncovers a few tiny grey fingers. I hold my breath. The forefinger moves, a tiny wriggling worm except there are no worms in this rubble. It's such a small movement. But it's movement. I start working more carefully now. Still as quick, but with a delicacy I usually reserve for my embroidery. Before I know it, there's a whole arm, part of a chest, and I can see the miracle of breathing in this tiny body. I clear where I now know the face is, and the baby blinks at the light. As we lift her out, we shout to the others, and I get a distinct sensation like milk letting down.

"Got a baby here! Can someone get some milk please? And a blanket and a fresh nappy?"

We're laugh-crying and holding her away from us as the nappy falls off her, encrusted with shit, rubble and wee. She must have been under there for at least twelve hours. She gives us a lopsided smile, and despite the fact she's covered in excrement and brick dust and concrete, I kiss her lovely little face. I'm trembling, and it's like I'm expanding so I don't know where I begin and end.

After we hand her over to the ambulance crew, Hilda and I decide we've done our bit for today, and I invite her back to mine for a cuppa. Turns out she's a pacifist, which surprises me.

"So why were you helping to clear the rubble today, then?" I bite my lip. "Sorry."

"That's OK. Valid question." She has the loveliest smile. I don't feel such an idiot when she smiles like that. We're women in it together, after all.

"It's something I *can* do. You see, I could never work in a munitions factory. Luckily, I don't have to, being a married woman and well over thirty. Mind you, I think that will change. They're going to need more and more women's labour to keep the war machine going, if you ask me. But even if they did call me up, I wouldn't do anything that perpetuated the war—only things that relieve suffering. Sorry. I'm rambling on."

"Oh, no!" I don't want her to stop. She's the first person I ever heard express a different opinion from what I hear on the wireless and read in the newspapers. Listening to her, I feel all tingly.

"Please. Don't stop. It's just—well, I've never met a pacifist before. Is that the right word? I don't wish offence."

"None taken. Yes. I'm a Quaker. I worship at Blackheath." Hilda looks at me, hands in lap, waiting for me to make the next move. But I chicken out.

"Oh gosh, is that the time? My kids'll be home soon, and I've done nothing about tea. Chips and one egg each it is, then!" I force a laugh. "See you tomorrow, I expect?" I don't want to let go of her, strange though she is. I want to know more. She isn't—well—run-of-the-mill.

Thinking about that baby, separated from its mama, has brought it all back. How Mama let go of me when the nasty white man and the white lady with long nails came and took me away. I remember Mama's arms going limp as I desperately tried to cling to her dress, my fingers being prized open, the cloth slipping out of my hands, the smell of Mama receding, overpowered by a strange scent that never grew in any forest. I hoped never again to feel so alone.

As I made tea, pulling my woollie round my chest, I cried for the little baby, for the little girl that was me, and for myself now with no parents and no Stan to hold onto.

Anyway, that's decided me. It's time to tell my Stan about the baby.

11ᵗʰ November 1940

I've decided to write to you, my imagined reader, as if you were my Mama. The Mama I dream about when I'm not having nightmares. Maybe one day you'll read this, Mama. I know if you were here, you'd help me get through this awful bloody mess, so I'm going to conjure you up and make you real for me. As if you were just a few miles away, and I was writing you letters until I could see you again.

What's decided me is, last night, I came to see you, Mama. Maybe it happened because it's upset me, thinking about stuff I'd buried long ago, like how it felt to be taken from you. Last night, I didn't feel upset — at first.

I can see you weaving a basket, sitting by the servants' fire in the big old house. I recall basket weaving at school here in England. The teacher couldn't understand why I was so good at it. I used to just smile and say nothing. Now, watching you, I'm back in the cocoon of my early childhood, feeling as if I could fall asleep by you as you work, just like countless times before. My body feels warm, as if a golden ray of late spring sunlight is warming me from the inside. I never want this moment to end.

I begin helping. You're working on a basket for a new baby. I'm not sure whose baby this is, but I try to make my fingers remember the old movements, conscious that I'm not as good at this as I once was. I prepare the flax, soaking it in water to soften it. We work silently. You know I know what to do; you don't need to tell me. We work all day — all of my night. When it's finished, you set it to one side and tell me, your eyes shining like two stars in my night:

"Tomorrow, we will begin making the mattress, and then the rest of the baby's bedding."

I feel my chest swell with pride at being able to help. I feel connected not only to you, but to my people. It feels right and good.

But then I wake up and realise I'm in London, all alone without you, bombs falling all around and the late autumn chill sneaking between the sheets, robbing me of the warmth I'd known just seconds before, with you. I sob into my pillow.

12th November 1940

When I read that last bit, I feel like shaking myself. I need to pull myself together. Stiff upper lip and all that.

It must be getting to me. I've gone all soft. Rescuing that baby the other day, and being reminded of what happened to me when I was little has left me brooding about it, so I'll use this diary to get things off my chest. I hope you don't mind, Mama. Then, maybe I can just forget about it and get on with sorting out how the kids and I are going to cope with Stan away, and another one likely to join us in a few months.

When I realised I wasn't ever going back home, I was left in a state of blind terror. Grieving for you, you might say, I was expected to call a new lady Mummy, and to get used to having a Daddy. They seemed to want me. They kept smiling at me without any provocation, but I just stood there staring. I was desperate to find a way back to you, Mama. I didn't want to shape those English words. They tasted like poison. And so, I didn't speak. What was the point in talking? I didn't know much English anyhow, and no one was going to talk our language, were they? I cried for months after I was taken from you, but always on my own. When I was with Mummy and Daddy, I stayed brave and well behaved, apart from the not talking, which I now know must have driven them mad with worry.

I must have put them through hell. They were kind people. But now they're dead, bits of their bodies thrown all over the place, or trapped forever in rubble, to be flattened when this war is over. I feel desperately alone, with no Mama, no Mum or Dad, and no Stan.

I don't think I can write any more about how I came to live in England. Not today. It's making me cry, and that just won't do. I've got to get the kids' tea on.

14th November 1940

I've sent the letter to Stan, Mama. I've no idea how he'll react. We both thought we'd completed our family, what with the French letters and all. I daresay he'll blame me for it not working.

Last night was a bad one. The bombs kept on falling throughout the night, all around us. I thought of those poor souls who'd been hit, and lay awake wondering, like I always do, if we'd be next. As usual, I soaked my sheets with sweat. I go to bed fully clothed these days, for fear I'll be up in the night, out on the streets. My overcoat lies over my bedding, keeping us warm and ready in case I need it. I've rehearsed being bombed out more times than I've had hot dinners. Grab the kids, get Adam and Henry to look after the other two. Gather blankets and overcoats (all the kids' coats are over us, but poor Adam's growing out of his and I haven't the money or coupons to get him another one). Shoes if we can find them. Maybe I should put the kids to bed in their shoes and wear mine, too. It's better than chilblains, or frostbite. Once we're out on the street, we run to the community shelter. It isn't far away — just opposite the Co-op. The men worked hard on building that shelter, even as Chamberlain was waving his useless bit of paper.

People round here have mostly painted a V-for-victory sign on their front walls, along with the Morse code of three dots and a dash. Even my old mate Shirley's done it. I wish I felt that gung-ho, Mama, but I can't bring myself to go through the motions. No doubt some people are pointing the finger at me behind my back. I can't help feeling for those poor ruddy pilots, especially during the Battle of Britain back in July. We could see planes in flames, above us. You had to keep an eye out and make sure you weren't where they were coming down, crashing in clouds of smoke and flames. One poor pilot ejected from his spitfire but was shot by a Jerry plane. He was dead by the time he hit the ground. I stood there watching, my legs threatening to give way. Some poor woman's son. Some kid's dad, maybe. Someone's husband or beau, perhaps.

Last night, the Murphys up the road had a lucky escape. They woke to find a few tiles missing. Apparently, a bomb had bounced off their roof, landed in the garden and burned itself out. Charmed lives. Irish. We've had a few bombs land in the woods behind our house. One lifted the Anderson shelter up the other night, so it's not secure anymore. When that fell, the windows rattled so much I thought they'd fall out. Maybe the blackout tape held them together, I don't know. I'd better get the Anderson shelter fixed in case we need it, though who I'll get to help me I don't know. Most of the men are away fighting this blasted war, and none of us girls were raised knowing how to wield a hammer. Mind you, I'm told you can get bunks put in, if you want. I'll have a word with the ARP warden.

Schools have been hit, too. The Brown School over on the common has had part of its structure blown away. I think those girls are going down to Maidstone in Kent, to continue their schooling there. I just hope my kids' school doesn't get hit. I can't be doing with four boys under my feet all day long.

16th November 1940

For some unknown reason, I confided in Hilda the day before yesterday about a few things. I mean, I haven't known her five minutes, and I told her things I've never told anyone, not even Shirley. God alone knows what made me go shouting my mouth off to her. I suppose I thought she seemed like a decent sort of person. With her being a Quaker, I probably hoped she might not think too badly of me. I didn't tell her everything—just that I wasn't born in England, and that I was adopted. I probably muttered something about being from an inferior race. At school, they were always going on about people with dark skins not being as intelligent as white people, and not as clean or civilized. So, I don't think I'm as good as other people, despite scrubbing away at my steps like the best of them and passing all my exams to go to grammar school. The only reason I didn't go was that Mum and Dad couldn't afford it. Uniforms and books cost money—money they didn't have. So, I just stayed on at elementary school, marking time. But when I told Hilda, do you know what she said, Mama? She said we're all equal in the eyes of God. Funny that. The church my Mummy and Daddy worshipped at didn't exactly say that. They kept on about savages in faraway places that needed saving. I was never quite sure what from.

I like Hilda. I suppose you could say she's becoming a friend. It's strange how now there's a war on, people seem to talk that wouldn't have given each other the time of day before. I'd have thought, before all these shenanigans, she was a bit too la-di-da for my liking. I'd probably have said unkind things about her. But yesterday, I had her round again, for a cuppa. I kept apologizing for the chipped cups, but she didn't seem to mind. In fact, she was very chatty and stayed about an hour and a half until she had to go, and my kids were due back from school. You'd like her, Mama. A white woman, of course, but very nice.

Actually, I've met a woman with darker skin, like mine. Her mother was born in India of all places. One of the countries where the church minister thought we should be saving "savages" like her. Mind you, she could pass for white. Very fine features. Her name's something unpronounceable. I call her Sandy, because it sounds a bit like that. I met her, and a nice Jewish woman called Ruth who's also quite dark, when I went to something Hilda had invited me to—a meeting of women who are against the war. I don't really know why I went because I can't be against the war. That Hitler needs to be stopped, with what he's doing to anyone he doesn't like. Apparently, a lot of people have it in for the Jews, not just in Germany. Why them? What have they ever done to us? Poor sods. I did know about the Black Shirts, of course, in the East End. Nasty pieces of work, all of them. Thugs, if you ask me. But what I didn't know was that as long ago as 1933 the Germans were putting Jews out of business. Then, there was that horrific Kristallnacht, in '38, which I knew about. The night of broken glass. That's when it got violent. Ordinary people thinking it was OK to torch Jews' places of worship and vandalise their homes and shops. Probably all good Christians, who went back to their families after a nice night torching Jewish homes. Ruth tells me about a hundred people died that night. Apparently, the Germans have now forced the Polish Jews into a ghetto in Warsaw, where they have fewer rations than the ordinary Poles and are basically starving to death. The latest is, the authorities go round shooting Jews. It makes my blood boil. No. I can't be a pacifist, whatever Hilda says. And I doubt Ruth can, either. Don't know about Sandy. Still, it's nice to meet some other women who, like me, are a bit different. Not that my neighbours treat me as different. I've always told people my dark looks were from Celtic ancestry. They've had no cause to believe different.

Money's so tight, I might have to pawn my engagement ring soon. At least I have one. Stan's a good man.

18th November 1940

The worst has happened. Well, maybe not the worst, but nearly as bad as it gets, Mama. Last night, I put the kids to bed under the table as usual, wearing their shoes and with their coats over the top of the blankets, then I sat nearby listening to the wireless. It was about nine o'clock. I'd just finished listening to the news about how we were pushing on in North Africa. I wish they could give me news about my Stan. I haven't heard from him for weeks. Don't know if he's dead or alive. Anyway, my mind was on other things, like how the heck am I going to give these kids any kind of Christmas. Suddenly, I'm thrown halfway across the room. I panicked. My first thought was the kids and how I must find them all and get them out. I've never been so glad to hear them crying. At least that meant they were alive, but I think I saw Stephen thrown up in the air and hit his head on the oak table. He was screaming, just sitting there, his little face all screwed up and looking helpless. That set David off wailing, so he reached his arms out for me. Henry cried too, more quietly, but Adam just rubbed his eyes and looked around, ready to spring into action to help me, bless him. He's too young to have so much on his shoulders. My oldest boy isn't getting the childhood that's rightfully his.

While all this happened in slow motion, glass poured into the room, covering the floor, and there was an almighty draft. Then a red light. Fire!

I think me having rehearsed helped, despite me being a bag of nerves. I told Adam and Henry to grab the little ones and follow me, gathering up the coats and blankets and my handbag as I groped my way towards the front door. I figured if the back of the house was on fire, the front should be OK. But I was trembling so much, I dropped my handbag and had to go down on hands and knees to get it. I wasn't losing my ration book and coupons! It's funny what becomes important at times like that. I told Adam to stay by the door and not open it. Once I was sure the kids were all out of the living room, I closed the door to keep the fire from spreading too quickly. Then I told Adam to open the front door. I gave them all instructions to be careful going down the steps, but of course Henry tripped holding the little one, so more crying and two nasty grazed knees. Thank God that was all. We ran to the community shelter. It seemed to take forever, but at least we were safe.

I didn't realise, until we all got to the communal shelter and saw Shirley there. She told me I had blood pouring down the side of my face and arms. The kids were unharmed, despite Stephen's bang on the head. Just shocked really. But being in the middle of the room, I got the flying glass. One of the ARP women in the shelter attended to me. Nice woman. Very quietly efficient, like she'd obviously got glass out near someone's eye before. I told her what happened, and she just nodded. No doubt she's heard the same story, many times. It stung when she put the Acriflavine on. I've got nice yellow patches all over my skin now! Very becoming.

After the all-clear went, the warden said she'd find us temporary accommodation. God alone knows when I will make it back to our street. I still haven't stopped shaking. I'm praying they won't stick us in temporary housing with loads of other families, where it takes forever to be rehoused. If there's a God up there, he'd better be listening.

20th November 1940

Well, maybe there is a God, Mama, and maybe it's a kind of birthday present. I'm thirty-one today, and it's my eleventh wedding anniversary. Not that I'm celebrating.

Anyhow, they've put us in with Ruth and her husband, Nathan, plus two children, Rebecca and Chaim (I had to ask how to spell that one!). They've got a tiny house down on Speranza Street. Not enough room to swing a cat, but they welcomed us with open arms. I've never met a man like Nathan. He comes home shattered, but when he sees Rebecca and Chaim, his big brown eyes twinkle like the stars in winter up on Shooters Hill. Then he sits in his chair, holds out his arms and lets them climb all over him. The way he holds them, you'd think they were the most precious things on God's earth. It's like watching someone with the most expensive silk, enjoying the feel and trying not to spoil it. I've never seen a man so obviously in love with his wife, either—the way he looks at her would melt me, I tell you. He even helps Ruth fill the tin bath, then kneels beside the little ones, pouring water on their backs and splashing and laughing. Then he wraps them in one of their threadbare towels, cradling them with such tenderness. They have to share a towel, so he gets one child out, gives them a quick dry, then the other—all the time singing something Yiddish.

They're very devout, too, Mama. They have Chanukah just before Christmas, when they light candles on this thing called a menorah that holds several thin candles. They give presents, not just once, but several days running. Of course, presents are in short supply, but they make things. Kids are always looking for bits of shrapnel, so Nathan gets a hammer and beats the metal into a shape. He's even made us something; a soap container we can take with us when we go back. For some reason it brought tears to my eyes. It's only an old lump of metal beaten into shape. But still.

They only have two bedrooms, not that anyone sleeps in their beds these days. They have a decent Anderson, so the family sleeps there, and I do my old trick of moving their table up against the main wall in the house.

Ruth and I get along so well. She hums to herself all day long, a half-smile on her face. She's taught me a song from Russia, though I've no idea whether I am pronouncing the words right or what the heck I'm singing. Apparently, Russia is where their parents came from. Both her and Nathan's parents came over in the early part of the century, during what's called a pogrom. It's another one of those times when Jews were persecuted for no good reason. Ordinary Russian people, after Jewish blood. Both Ruth's and Nathan's parents managed to get some money together so they could leave Russia and come to Britain. I think the families had some saved, and they had a few valuables. Heirlooms. But they had to leave the older relatives behind. They told the young people to go. Imagine being told to go and get out so that you could start a new life, have kids, and carry on the family name, knowing the people who were telling you to do that risked death as they gave you all they had. It doesn't bear thinking about. Some of Ruth's family went to America, so they've got cousins there, though no hope of ever seeing them, I daresay.

Anyway, enough of being all sad. Today, Ruth and me baked a cake. She's got this ration cookbook. Of course, sugar's in short supply but we used golden syrup, and it tasted lovely. A treat for Nathan and the kids when they came home. Nathan's not been called up yet. He's a tailor. I think he's hoping maybe he can be used to make uniforms and such like, rather than go and fight. He doesn't look like a fighter to me.

I shall miss the Goldbergs when our house is repaired. I expect they'll just board up where the windows were and have us back in there. It'll be even darker than before. The lean-to looked to be shattered, so we won't have that anymore. I just hope I've got a working kitchen to go back to. But I'm not really looking forward to it. It's nice, having another woman to share the day with and work alongside. We rub along really well, Ruth and I.

I hadn't had a bath since I came to Ruth's house. Baths are once a week, on Saturday in our house. I have a strip wash most days. Of course, being bombed out, we were all filthy. I don't like to use their hot water, and I wouldn't want to get in the bath when Nathan's around. But Ruth suggested today she and I take a bath together, so we heated the water and poured it into the tin bath, and in we got! I didn't use too much soap. Just enough to get rid of the dirt. And of course, with two of us in there we didn't need as much water either. It felt strange, getting in together. I couldn't help my knees rubbing up against hers, though at first, I was trying to avoid it, and I felt shy being naked in front of her. But she was so relaxed it helped. She asked me to soap her back. Such velvety skin. We ended up rolling about laughing, splashing each other. I haven't had so much fun in ages. She shared her towel with me.

I'm definitely going to miss Ruth, when we go back home.

25th November 1940

We're back in our house! Of course, it needed a thorough clean, and most of the windows have, as predicted, just been boarded up, making it very dark. There's a gap where the lean-to was, but the door's in one piece. There was loads of debris and dust, which is going to take weeks to completely get rid of.

It feels quiet when the kids are at school. I haven't felt like doing much today. I got the washing and housework done, and cooked for the kids, but at lunchtime I didn't bother eating. I went round the Links—the Co-op—where Ruth, Hilda and Sandy were making boards to hold up. Why they want to demonstrate against the war beats me. I think they're very brave, though. People will spit at them and call them names. I said to Ruth:

"Why are you against this war? The Germans are trampling all over Jewish people!"

She smiled at me, not in a kind of "how can you be so stupid" way but looking all serene. Then she said—she whose parents had to escape persecution, mind:

"It's not the ordinary Germans, Aggie. It's the Nazis. The people's minds are being poisoned, but that doesn't mean we should kill."

"But hang on," I says, being clever. "Don't you say an eye for an eye?"

"That's often misunderstood, Aggie. Forgive me. I don't mean to—
"

She squirmed. I got the feeling she was worried if she went on lecturing me, I would feel like the uneducated so-and-so I am. But she carried on, anyway.

"Moses was given that guidance, so that the punishment should fit the crime. But we're also told we mustn't take vengeance or hold grudges."

Then she looked at me straight, like she didn't care anymore what I thought about her little speech.

"We shouldn't punish a whole people, Aggie."

I felt a right fool. I remember my parents reading the bible to me, and as soon as I was old enough, I had to read a chapter a night. But I never actually studied it and thought about it. Ruth clearly has. Well, the Old Testament anyway. She's obviously a well-educated lady, despite their humble means, unlike me. Still, at least I can read and write pretty well. I was good at English at school.

Anyway, it hasn't made enemies of us. Ruth's lent me a book. It was lovely to cuddle up next to the kids, all warm and snug with a book in my hands this evening. I don't think I've done that since *What Katy Did Next*. This one's called *The Age of Innocence* and it's by an American called Edith Wharton. It's gripping. All about falling in love with the wrong person. I'm glad my life isn't as complicated.

Meanwhile, the new little one inside me is making himself felt. I'm about four months and getting regular kicks now. The sickness has finally died down, thank God; it went on longer than usual. I looked in the mirror today, and my skin and eyes look the picture of health. I would have been blooming before now, if it hadn't been for being bombed out. It's a wonder it didn't bring on a miscarriage. Like I say, my babies are obstinate, Mama.

Oh, and I got a letter back from Stan. Typical man. He says he's delighted I'm pregnant again, but hopes it's a girl. As if I can order one!

26th November 1940

Stephen's got a temperature. I've kept him off school. He's really listless—and it's like he's on fire. I've sent Adam to see if Hilda's got any ideas. I think Hilda has some First Aid training. I'm soaking old rags in cold water and fanning him to bring the temperature down. I'm worried, I don't mind admitting.

Later, same day

Hilda says I've got to get him to the doctor, toot sweet. She'll stay with the other kids. His breathing sounds really bad now, and he has purple blotches on his skin she held a glass to. Said something about meningitis. I'm writing this, wrapping him up in an old towel, and running.

28th November 1940

I'll have to put this diary on hold. God alone knows why I got all airs and graces and thought about writing, when I should've been doing my job as a mother.

My beautiful boy, Stephen—my baby—died in my arms yesterday morning, as dawn was breaking. I'm living in a nightmare. Maybe soon I'll wake up and that precious boy will be alive again, running round and knocking into things and falling over and getting up to no good. I'd give anything to have him back. He could be as naughty as he liked. I wouldn't even tell him off. Just hold him tight and tell him I love him, which I didn't do enough of.

I've never wished more that Stan was here. Another letter came today. I can't be bothered to copy what he said. It doesn't matter. Nothing matters now. I need my head to stop spinning and I need to stop vomiting bile. I just keep staring into space. I haven't even got the kids' tea. Our Adam got some bread and butter and jam for them all, which they swilled down with tea and Tate and Lyle. They went to bed good as gold. At least, thanks to Adam, they had full tummies. I'm sitting in the dark. I don't even want to light a candle. The planes are doing their usual all around me, and I haven't the energy to get under the table. Now there are three. Oh, God, take me tonight and put me out of my misery. Mama, if you can see this, please give me a hug. I so need a hug from you right now. I don't feel big enough to deal with this all on my own.

Now I must write to Stan. I've only just told him he's going to be a father yet again, now I have to tell him one of his sons is dead. How the hell do you tell a man that, when he's far from home, fighting to stay alive himself?

5th December 1940

The funeral was a simple affair. Just me, the kids, the priest, and Hilda came even though it's not her church. I felt as if it wasn't really me in my body as I stood there, mouthing the words to hymns and prayers like I used to as a girl. Hilda kept her arm round me, which was just as well as I have no idea how I stayed upright. I was glad when it was over, and everyone had gone home, and the kids were safely tucked up, and I could sit alone with my thoughts. I didn't cry all day. I was too numb to cry, but our Adam kept sniffing and blowing his nose, bless him. You don't realise how these things affect children, do you? Of course, he set Henry off, then David started though he didn't know why, clinging to my legs. My brother David is staying in the countryside and decided not to make the journey.

There was an autopsy. He did have meningitis. Just one of those things, they said. It could have happened any time, not just in war. I'm still numb, but I must keep going, for the kids. I seem to float through each day like someone possessed. I don't cry, not until the kids are in bed. Then, I sit in the old rocker, holding my bump as if he was the one inside me.

Last night, I came to you, Mama.

You look as beautiful as ever, Mama—still young, but a bit older than when I visited you last. I wonder if this can be real, because you never seem to be as old as you should be now. But I dismiss the thought, not wanting anything to drag me back, away from you.

There's something else to keep me here, tonight. Next to you, sitting up to the table in the servants' quarters, is Stephen. It's obvious from how easily he chats away to you about nothing, the way little boys do, and the way his body leans into you as you reach over to give him another little titbit, that he knows you, and you know him, as if you'd always been together. In front of him are cakes, biscuits, and milk. A feast for a little boy who, until very recently, was on rations. I watch as his little chubby fingers reach and grab a biscuit, shoving it whole into his mouth as fast as he can, just in case a brother appears from nowhere to snatch it. He turns his face up to you, smiling with those little dimples either side of his mouth, and his cheeks look glowing with health, stuffed full of biscuit he has not yet been able to swallow down. I know I can trust you with him. You are his grandmother. You stroke the top of his head as you lean over, refilling his cup of milk. I know, looking at the way you are with him, that despite you looking so young you have other grandchildren. I slip in beside you, and you pour me a cup of tea. It's as if we do this every day—you, me and Stephen. There's a feeling of companionship, the bond between mothers as we sit at the table and drink tea, chatting about this and that. It feels so normal. Like being wrapped up in a favourite old coat, warm and snug. Then something makes me look up. Outside the window, noisy fireworks light up the sky. They must be celebrating something. But then I'm dragged backwards, with an overwhelming force.

I woke up, my guts twisted inside me as the baby kicked, blissfully unaware she has already lost a brother. I curled up in a ball and howled. The kids slept on beside me, and the deadly fireworks continued, too close for comfort.

6th December 1940

A social worker came to call today. They say I should think about evacuating to Stan's uncle and aunt in Yorkshire. I haven't the energy to do the housework, let alone move. All those dark satanic mills. I can see it getting me down more than the bombs. But I know I should do it, for the children.

I suppose I should be pleased we aren't just being sent to God knows who, but I've never even met Stan's relations. They might be horrible people, for all I know. Assuming we're still there after the baby's born, how will they like being woken all hours of the day and night? I'll think about it. I've heard Jerry takes a pop at evacuees' trains, as well. Not sure I want to make myself and my kids a sitting target for them. Mind you, if I'm going, it'd better be soon. I can't be making the move when I'm eight and a half months pregnant, or with a new baby that's for sure. And there's no knowing when this awful Blitz will end.

7th December 1940

I don't know why, but I had a terrible thought, about my father. I suddenly realised he was the man you worked for, wasn't he? I just hope he didn't force himself on you. I want to believe that every time you looked at me you saw not the horror that made me, but love. Did you love him, Mama? Did he love you? Did you both love me?

8th December 1940

I wasn't going to write again. Not when I've lost my little boy and my husband is off God knows where, serving his country. But it helps, a bit like a trouble shared is a trouble halved. And who knows? Maybe one day this record will be of use to someone, to know what we all went through in these terrible times.

I went upstairs this morning, looking for a scarf for David. I don't want him being ill. I'm terrified I'll lose another child. With him being now my youngest, I'm watching him like a hawk. Mind you, he's quite clingy, so there's not much chance of me losing him from my sight. Oh, and they've stopped Stephen's coupons. So that's that. Less for us all to eat. Anyway, I'm getting sidetracked as usual. Butterfly brain, my mum used to call me. Worse than ever, what with the pregnancy and being upset making it impossible to think straight. When I went upstairs, I noticed a cupboard door ajar, to where I keep the little bit of jewellery I've got—stuff my mum passed on to me, like an emerald ring and a gold cross. I hadn't noticed it was open before, what with all that's been going on. I'm wracking my brains to think what else was there. Anyway, you can probably guess what's coming next. I've been cleared out of all my special things. It's not the monetary value, though thinking about it, I'm skint, and they might have brought pawn money. It's that I have precious little from my mum and dad. Apart from what they'd already passed on to me and my brother, everything was lost in the rubble. And now, even those things I did have are gone. What kind of person would want to kick you when you're down? The gangsters are having a field day, being given free access to property right now. Nothing's sacred. Nothing. So, now I've lost my parents, my boy, and my precious things. I feel like a raft, floating out to sea in the middle of nowhere. But every now and then I hit rocks, and I have to come to and make tea.

9th December 1940

I can hold out no longer, what with the expense of having buried my darling boy. I've pawned my engagement ring. I won't tell Stan. It would break his heart. That's it. I've now hit rock bottom.

10th December 1940

The social worker has been in touch with Stan's relations, Margaret and Harold. She says it's all fixed. We're moving to Yorkshire after Christmas. I don't remember agreeing to it, but I haven't got the energy to argue. One less family for her to worry about.

11ᵗʰ December 1940

Hilda and Ruth have each been round, bringing food for us from their rations, so that I don't have to cook just now. Good, reliable old Shirley also visited, bringing a Lancashire hotpot freshly cooked and steaming for the kids' and my tea. She didn't stop long. She looked awkward, eyes darting around and looking anywhere but at me. Made some excuse about needing to visit an elderly aunt. Despite her being my oldest friend, I doubt I'll be seeing her again any time soon. I gave most of the hotpot to the kids. I didn't feel much like eating. I wish I could say I appreciated the company, but it's such an effort to act normal. I know they don't expect me to. Hilda and Ruth both said as much. But I feel I've got to entertain. Sandy came today. I've found out her real name, by the way. I like to know people's real names, even though I don't tell anyone mine. She's Sandhya. Lovely name. It means twilight apparently. And get this! She's a Catholic! So, I'm now friends with a Quaker, a Jew and a Catholic. One white, two different shades of brownish, like me. I can't seem to make myself go to church, even though Mum and Dad were keen to bring me and David up as true believers. Theirs was a very high church—a bit like the Catholics, actually, Mama. You wouldn't have liked it. Bad enough it was that the bosses made us go to church every Sunday, when I was with you. But I suppose it stood me in good stead because I knew who Jesus was by the time I came to England.

The Quakers are funny. They don't have priests. They say anyone can listen to God, a bit like tuning in the wireless, and find out what he wants of them. They sometimes feel so compelled to stand up and say something in their religious meetings they shake, which is how they got the name Quakers. The proper name of their church is the Religious Society of Friends. They're big on the fellowship side and on treating everyone as equals. I might go one day, when I'm feeling a bit better. God knows I need someone to hold my hand and lead me through this darkness.

12th December 1940

I went down the market today. Sandy—Sandhya—said it might do me good. I stopped at a jewellery stall for some reason, and there, right in front of me, was my emerald ring. My voice got caught in its box like a bird in a chimney, covered in soot. I clutched at my burning throat, and my head went all swimmy. Sandy must have noticed something, because she held onto my arm and asked if I was alright. She sat me down and got a glass of water off the stallholder that sells tea. The baby did a somersault. My ring, there in broad daylight.

After that, Sandy and me went up to the community hall and told Ruth and Hilda. Ruth looked cross—asked why I didn't just grab it off the stallholder. Hilda looked thoughtful.

"I doubt very much the stallholder was the one who took it. Might not even be the fence. She was probably told it belonged to someone who died, and the family needed the money."

Her voice was gentle, like she was breaking it to me in small bites. Then she turned to the others:

"Look, ladies. This might be a bitter pill to swallow, but when have you knowingly bought stockings that fell off the back of a lorry?"

We all looked at each other, waiting for someone else to speak first. It didn't need answering. The black market is as alive and kicking as the baby in my tummy. I think from now on I'm going to start drawing a line up the back of my legs, no matter how cold it's got.

But what I'm going to do for Christmas, I have no idea.

13th December 1940

Hilda had a nice idea. She's got hold of some rags. She knows how to make rag rugs. She's going to teach me how, so I can make one for each of the kids, for Christmas. They can sleep on it or have it over them. I'll have to stay up late a few times, if I'm going to make them in time for Christmas Day. When you're pregnant, that's not such a clever idea. Mind you, having something to do with my hands might pull me out of this pit I'm stuck in. I don't know why, but my hands feel the pain more than any other part of me. They need to keep busy. Maybe I'll make really quick meals for the rest of the time leading up to Christmas Day. The kids will have to see me making the rugs. I'll say they're for someone who's been bombed out. I've managed to get some bright colours—reds, and yellows and greens. The kids will love that. I've got to snap out of this, for their sakes. I'm hoping to get a nice bit of fish for Christmas day and bake some biscuits. I can't get hold of a turkey, and I'm not going to buy one off the black market. I can't afford their exorbitant prices, and now I've seen how it works, I'm minded to steer clear. If I can.

14ᵗʰ December 1940

Well, I'm halfway through my first rag rug! They'll brighten the place up I must say! I think I'll learn quilting next. What's made me say that is, today was my lucky day, if such a thing exists anymore. A Red Cross parcel arrived all the way from Canada. I needed something to cheer me up a bit. I've been sent a lovely quilt made out of bits of old suits and backed with some grey flannel, filled with kapok I think it is. It's lovely and warm and stretches right across the four of us, keeping us toasty all night long—which is just as well, as it's turned very cold.

Jerry's still at it every night, but I've got used to it. Sounds daft, I know. No snow yet thankfully, but we've had some evil frosts. My shoes are wearing a bit thin, and I've lost the heel to one of my boots. The kids' shoes aren't much better, and all of us have legs so desperate for a bit of warmth that when I make the fire up and get a blaze going, we come out in big blotches sitting on the fender boxes or on an armchair right up against the hearth. Of course, our backs freeze even though we're almost on fire on our fronts. I just hope I don't get chilblains. I do love a roaring fire, though I don't light it until an hour before the kids go to bed, and I only top it up once, to save on coal. I sit here, watching it die down once the kids are in bed. Last night we did toast and dripping on it, with plenty of salt. The kids love that. It warms you from the inside, especially washed down with a nice cup of tea. It still feels like there's this gap though, where Stephen should be. Like a big gaping hole in my belly, right next to the baby I'm carrying. I don't think I'll ever get over it.

There's some warmth in the midst of my icy world. I got a letter today, from Stan. It was three pages long and I must have read it at least as many times. The kids all wanted to know what their dad had to say, so I read out the bits about them and some of the high jinks he's been getting up to. Apparently, he and another geezer stole some brandy from the officer's mess and handed it round among the ratings. They got a bit tipsy I think, but never got caught! Just as well. I don't want him being shot at dawn or whatever it is they do to them.

I didn't read the end of the letter out to the boys. It said:

> *I miss you so much, my darling. I can taste your lips in my dreams. How I long for some shore leave so that I can kiss you for real. I love you more than ever, my dearest. Write soon.*
>
> *All my love,*
> *Stanley*

It made me blush, reading that. But it helped me to sleep, knowing he loves me so much. Sometimes, people have to go away before you realise how much you love them.

He obviously hadn't yet got my letter about Stephen, though. How I wish we could cling to each other right now.

15ᵗʰ December 1940

I often wonder what your normal day is like, Mama. I would love to be a part of that. It's the little things I miss, like being able to brush your hair for you. Do you remember when I used to do that? I must have made a complete dog's dinner of it, but I thought I was making you look pretty. Anyway, I'll tell you about my typical day, since I'm trying to get back to whatever passes for normal in these wretched times. I can't be moping around when there's work to do, can I?

I wake around six. I like to be up and ready for the children. It takes a long time to get four - now three, God rest his little soul—children ready for school. I get all their clothes laid out the night before, but despite that there's often panic, as one boy or the other loses a sock or his underpants. I get the porridge on around 6:30, after I've had a lick and a promise at the sink. Time to get them up at 7:30. I get them to line up for a wash and a hair brush, and then they pull on their clothes, shivering and blinking. I sometimes have to sort David out as he inevitably puts a sock on inside out or has his cardigan buttoned up all wrong. But they all sit down to a nice hot breakfast. I'm not sending my kids to school without food in their tummies, even if it is only porridge made with half and half. My mum wouldn't have sent me off without being fed, and neither would you have done if you'd had me long enough to see me off to school, Mama. You'd be surprised at how some kids go to school round here. I daresay money's scarce for a lot of people.

I let Adam and Henry walk David to school, and then I get on with the chores. First the washing up, then sweeping floors and dusting, cleaning the privy—an even more unwelcome job at this time of year and a messy one. The kids often miss, no doubt because they're freezing their socks off and still half asleep as they queue up to use it, and sometimes two of them go in there at the same time if they're desperate, me calling out:

"Don't wee on your brother! I haven't got any more clean shorts!"

It needs doing every day, the lav. It's about half past ten by the time I've done all that, and what I do next depends on what day it is. I usually sit down for a cuppa (I eat my porridge with the kids), and then go and do a bit of shopping. I need to shop every day. I usually go down to Stubbins, the greengrocer's on the corner, for four pounds of spuds and a pound each of carrots and greens, if I can get them. Then after I've dropped that lot back home I go to the Links for my meat and groceries. I usually buy some flour to make my own bread. I'm always baking. And either a bit of fish or some sausages or mince—whatever I can get, for tea. A few eggs, maybe. I come back and make myself a boiled egg for lunch, or maybe cheese on toast, or if I can't be bothered to wait, a corned beef or spam sandwich. Then, if it's a Monday, it's washing day, and that takes all afternoon until the kids come in demanding their tea. I try and make a casserole on Mondays and some rice pudding, so I can shove it in the oven and leave it.

Tuesday is always ironing. But the rest of the week I sometimes skip the chores and go down to the Links hall to help out there. There's always a family in need. And lately I've been getting involved in the leafleting, letting people know war is wrong. Hilda's been explaining it all to me, and although I have yet to be convinced entirely, I am starting to change my tune on that one.

Of course, once the children are back from school, I feed them and read any letters the school has sent home, help them with their reading, light the fire, and then it's time to put them to bed once I've washed up and we've all listened to the wireless to see how their daddy is doing in the war. Once they're asleep, I get their clothes ready for the morning and read my book. I love reading, Mama.

I went along to Hilda's Quaker Meeting today, it being a Sunday. It's very different from what I was brought up with. No hymns, no prayers, no readings. Everyone sits in silence, and every now and then someone stands to speak, as the spirit moves them. I felt a bit like a fish out of water, if I'm honest.

I seem to recall you had a version of the Lord's Prayer you sang to me in our own language. I can't remember the words—just the sound and the feel of it. What I do remember is our belief in the power of the earth—and of the world of spirit. I know it exists. I know my spirit travels sometimes, without leaving this earth, and I like to think that's what I am doing when I come to you, Mama.

Anyway, life goes on here, though now of course I have the extra work involved in preparing for Christmas *and* a move. What to take, and what to leave behind, is the question. I don't hear nearly enough from Stan, but he writes when he can. I love my man, Mama. I've a feeling you would approve. He's a good man, honest as the day is long. And his big, strong arms make me feel safe. I do miss him.

18th December 1940

Mama, I came to see you last night. I wanted to talk to you about what that Lieutenant told me. You see, I can't and won't believe that my Stan has committed such a terrible crime.

I see you in the middle distance, walking along the beach by the big lake. I run to catch you up, then walk alongside you. Two women, walking together. This time, and the time before, I have a distinct sense of no longer being a little girl when I visit. And I see you as the age you really are. Don't ask me how, but I know I have brothers and sisters, and a stepfather. It's beyond my wildest dreams of course, but I wish one day to meet them and be accepted back into the great people I began my life with. My mind runs away with me, thinking maybe my boys could be accepted, too.

It's a lovely sunny summer's day, not like the midwinter's night I willingly left behind. You look beautiful, despite being twenty-seven years older than when I was taken. You must be in your late forties. Still that lovely black hair, now with silver streaks, and pinned up. You're as elegant as a gazelle (not that I've ever seen one, only in books). I'm just a little in awe of how magnificent a lady you look. And you have a parasol! It must come in handy. I'm squinting — the sun is so bright, reflected off the water. I look around and see a few more houses than when I lived here, but I can see our hill in the background. I'm struck by a sudden urge to visit that sacred place and tramp barefoot up its steep inclines, to savour the view from the summit! But I don't want to leave you. I focus on the sound of our feet crunching stones, the water lapping gently back and forth, the feeling of sun on my skin, the look of it dancing on the lake — a shared moment with you that I want to last for an eternity.

I hear you breathe in, in that way you always used to when you had something important to say.

"My darling daughter. You mustn't give up trying to clear your husband's name. Don't accept defeat."

Your eyes stay focussed forwards.

"And you have another job to do. You mustn't go under. You're needed."

I feel all at once puzzled, burdened, and intrigued, almost excited.

"What do you mean, Mama? What job?"

You turn towards me and smile. I recognise that look from when I was small. A look that says, "stop asking questions, and be patient."

That was when I was pulled back through the earth. I am, as always, left with a feeling of sadness at having lost you once again. Each time it happens, it's like that first time all over again. And I feel such a fool for entertaining thoughts of my children being accepted into our people. Even if I had the money to get on a boat with them and travel all that way, it would be difficult, with Stan not being one of us. I couldn't see him agreeing to upping sticks and going to the other side of the world, though some have, I know. Despite speaking the same language in the same accent as everyone around me, I feel apart, somehow. I can't explain to anyone how important the ancestors are to me. Or the land. When I hang the washing out, I touch the earth, knowing it's the same earth as my ancestors trod, and that you still tread, Mama, even if it is on the other side of the world.

Just how I'm meant to clear my old man's name beats me. Oh, Mama, I want to go to my husband, to tell that blasted Royal Navy they've got it all wrong. But I'll look and wait. Look and wait. I must remember my dignity. Besides, I have my boys to think about, and this unborn child of mine. They need me, too. Maybe that's what you meant, Mama, when you said I am needed. Only time will tell.

19th December 1940

Today, I wrote Stan a letter. I've copied it out here, because I want to make sure if it goes astray as I fear it might, that I can refer to it. I might have left school at fourteen, but I'm not stupid. There were many like me, bright girls and boys deprived of a decent education for want of a few bob. People who now work in shops and clean houses, hospitals and schools, but could have been teachers, or doctors or even big shot lawyers, if only their parents had had the money for all the necessaries.

I'm beginning to wonder whether I've spent too many years following what my parents taught me about accepting your lot in life. This is what I wrote:

My darling Stanley,

I miss you every day, and the boys do too.

I had a visit from a Lieutenant Arthur Wright. I wrote down the details of our conversation after I showed him the door, so as not to forget it. He seemed a nice man. He'd been sent, or at least allowed to come, by the Commander of your ship to tell me what you're accused of.

I know you would never do such a vile and violent thing. I told him you wouldn't harm a fly. Even when there's a spider in the lav, I'm the one to get it and flush it down. You'd rather leave it where it is.

Stan, we're going to fight this. I'm certain you're covering for someone, or maybe you've been framed.

I've been told I can't come out there to see you, but I've spoken to my friend Sandhya, who was born in India by the way. I tend to call her Sandy because it's easier, but I suppose

62

I should use her proper name, by rights. Her old man is a lawyer called d'Souza. I can't believe I'm mixing with a lawyer's wife, but it takes all sorts, and this war throws people together that would never have given each other the time of day before. The name sounds more Spanish than Indian to me, but she tells me it's Portuguese. Apparently, they—the Portuguese that is—invaded that bit of India where he's from. They're Catholics.

But I'm going all round the houses, as usual. I'm no better at getting to the point than I was before you went away, am I? I know it used to frustrate the hair off your head. I'm sorry, love. But maybe it'll make you laugh. God knows you must need that right now.

Anyway, this d'Souza chap has some connection to the Indian Navy, which of course is linked to ours. Apparently, some of the Indian men aren't entirely happy to be fighting for us. There have been "incidents." Sandy—Sandhya—says she'll ask her husband if he can do anything to help.

I hope they don't prevent you getting this letter. No doubt bits will be torn or blacked out.

Anyway, know that I love you just as much as you love me, and—this might surprise you, knowing how I've always hidden behind my mum, or you—I'm not taking this lying down. Stay strong.

Your ever-loving

Aggie xx

It's gone. I posted it this morning.

20th December 1940

Mama, there are children here in England who, like me all those years ago, have had to leave their mothers behind. Different reason—worse. I didn't know until Ruth and Hilda told me. Apparently, some Quakers have been involved in helping them.

The Quakers set up something called the Germany Emergency Committee in 1933, shortly after Hitler came to power. Then, after Kristallnacht just over two years ago, when loads of people went round killing Jews and burning their places of worship and so on, Hilda tells me six Quakers travelled to Berlin, to see things for themselves. Don't ever let anyone tell you those Quaker men who refuse to fight are yellow bellies. They're a plucky bunch. Apparently, these Quakers asked the British government if they could give the children visas to come to England. Then, they helped get the children out of Germany. The operation—called Kindertransport—officially ended the day we declared war on Germany and they, the Germans that is, stopped co-operating (they had been reluctant co-operators, mind). Despite the dangers, the last of these poor little mites arrived here via the Netherlands as late as May this year. But that's it, now. They can't get any more out.

Mama, Quakers went to accompany those children in the most horrible of conditions, their parents often not allowed to say goodbye to them in public, and the trains sealed. Once here, more Quakers took them in or found homes for them. I tell you, Quakers have definitely gone up in my estimation.

What Ruth and Hilda told me has got me thinking. I want to help those children, Mama. If I'd known about them sooner, I might have done more to help. After all, I know how it feels to lose the one person who makes you feel safe at night. At least your life wasn't in danger when I left, though. It makes me shudder. I'm lucky in a way. I have you to visit on my travels, and to write to here. I'm convinced you live and breathe, just across the other side of this big ball on which we sit. Those poor little things probably won't have any family to go back to after this dreadful business is over.

21st December 1940

Hilda thinks she might have a little Jewish girl for me to take in, who was initially sent to a farming family in Kent. The Quakers have been monitoring the placements for the children who came to this country. Apparently, this poor girl is twelve years old, hardly speaks a word of English, and was put to work on the farm from dawn to dusk. Hard physical work, anything from milking cows to scrubbing floors to lugging heavy sheets through a ringer. The couple complained this girl wasn't pulling her weight, so the Quakers removed her. They had a car, and when she got out of this car at the other end of the journey, they spotted a load of blood on the seat. The girl seemed to be limping and clutching her tummy. I'd have just thought she was getting the curse, but she must have looked poorly because they took her to a doctor who said she was losing a baby. Twelve years old and pregnant! Well, that's not ever likely to be her fault, is it? That pig of a farmer must have done it, or another boy or man on the farm. When I heard, I felt like punching his lights out.

I shall have to make her up a bed away from the boys, because it isn't proper to put a girl that age in with the opposite sex. Maybe she can sleep in the Anderson shelter, if we can get the ARP to fix it and put bunks in there. I'm sure she'll feel safer there, away from us. But I'll treat her like one of my own. She'll arrive just in time for Christmas. I do hope she doesn't mind us celebrating, what with her being Jewish and all that. She'll have to take us as she finds us. Her name, apparently, is Esther. I'll introduce her to Ruth, so she feels more at home.

Of course, she'll have to come with us when we go north. I've written to Uncle Harold and Auntie Margaret, and we'll see what they say.

23rd December 1940

Mr. d'Souza has been round to see me with Sandhya. He's such a charming man. So quietly spoken, and such nice manners. He stood when I stood. Very cultured. And clean. Nice white cuffs to his shirt, and silver cufflinks. I like a man that wears cufflinks.

Anyway, he says he'll write a letter on his lawyer's letterhead, to the Commander of the ship asking if he can be Stan's legal representative. He says it will be difficult, but worth a shilling. Not that he would take any money from me. It's just an expression. It was all I could do to stop myself from hugging him, but I got the feeling that would not be cricket! Of course, it's left me in such a two and eight all I can do is think and plan. I keep going over and over it as if it's me that has to talk to those toffs and make them see sense. It's just as well I have Esther coming tomorrow to take my mind off it. The ARP have been round and fixed the Anderson shelter and put bunks in. I'd better go and get things ready for her! I've been given an eiderdown and some sheets, and I had a spare blanket so hopefully she'll be OK.

26th December 1940

Christmas has been and pretty well gone.

Esther arrived, as planned, on Christmas Eve. Of course, it's not her holiday, but she was very gracious and didn't seem to mind us singing a few carols to cheer ourselves up. As she shook my hand, she announced in perfect English but with a thick accent:

"I shall call you Ma, if that's acceptable?"

I don't know if she'd been put up to it, but knowing her own mother may well have gone to meet her Maker, it choked me up.

We ran out of coal on Christmas Day. Bless her, Sandy had a bit to spare, and she knows I'll pay her back as soon as I can get some. I eked it out with some wood, after I'd sent the kids up to the woods on a hunt. They loved it, especially Esther, and all of them came back looking ruddy and healthy. I got them to pile it all up in the back garden.

I reckon I'm about five months gone now. Lots of kicks, and still enough room to breathe, which is just as well with this lot to look after. But I like having a girl around the place. I've given her a set of rags for her monthlies. It means more washing of course, but she can do her own rags and hang them out in the yard. The problem is at this time of year they'll go stiff with ice if we leave them out too long, so they'll have to come in and be hung over the fire guard, but at least they'll get an airing. I just hope we don't get our you-know-what at the same time once I give birth—not that I'm expecting it for a while. I'll be breastfeeding as long as possible. That'll keep it all at bay. And it delays having to go mushing stuff up and saves money and coupons. The children seem permanently hungry. I have memories of being allowed down into the kitchen and cook giving me little titbits, so maybe if I was permanently hungry, I didn't bother you as much as my kids bother me.

I sent Esther off to the shelter on Christmas Eve and put the rest of us to bed under the table as usual. I gave the poor girl a hug and kissed her on the cheek as I said goodnight, and she said, "Goodnight, Ma," looking so serious and forlorn. There's been little let-up in the bombing.

Still, we had a nice fish Christmas dinner. We had Christmas pud with the top off the milk, and by the end we were all stuffed! I got the silver threepenny bit—didn't mean it to be me, so I gave it to Adam, and then I gave them all their presents; I hadn't had time to make a rag rug for Esther, so she got the rags and some needles and thread to sew it all together with. I told her I'll show her how to make her own, miming to be sure she understood me. She seemed so pleased you'd think I'd given her the crown jewels! I took her round to meet Ruth and Nathan and their brood today. She looked so excited to be able to speak Yiddish with someone, I left them all to it and Ruth brought her round later, after giving her some tea and a small present of a knitted bracelet. It's Chanukah, you see, when they give presents every day for several days. Anyway, after Esther had gone off to fetch her book, Ruth had a word with me and told me that December 25th is in fact Esther's birthday! She's now thirteen years old.

While Esther was with Ruth and her family, some of us went to the community hall in the Links. We all took something we'd baked, and the kids had a lovely time running round. We played lots of games: blind man's buff, pin the tail on the donkey (someone drew a very good donkey on the back of a few Jerry leaflets stuck together) and such like. We sang loads of songs that the kids like, including, "Knees Up Mother Brown," and of course the "Hokey Cokey." By the end of it, I was dead on my feet, but in a good way.

Esther's turning out to be a real asset. With the kids being off school, I'm benefiting from her help a lot. She happily does a bit of sweeping and helps with the kids, and she's even done some baking. I don't want to over-use her, but then if I had a daughter, I'd be asking her to help around the house. The boys are useless, of course, but then every mother says the same, and I do wonder sometimes whether we mollycoddle our boys. Maybe if we expected them to help the way we do the girls, they'd come good. Who knows? I'm hoping to get Esther into school, so I can't have her to help all the time, but she's a good girl. Has terrible pains in her tummy, though. I wonder if it's got anything to do with what she's been through. She's a scrap of a thing. Needs feeding up. I'd give her larger portions, if we weren't rationed. Her cheeks look as if someone's taken a spoon and scooped them out.

Oh, and the Yorkshire relations have said it's OK for Esther to come with us. A bit of me was hoping they'd say no.

27th December 1940

I don't know how I am writing this. I can't feel my limbs or be sure not to fall over when I stand up. My hand is shaking, hence the scrawl, Mama. I can hardly breathe.

The dreaded day has arrived—the day I rehearsed but hoped would never come. The day I've seen other women go through and felt guiltily grateful it wasn't me.

Last night I had a dream. I, alone, was responsible for getting a load of people to safety from advancing water. I came to a point where I needed to make a decision. I froze, unable to tell which direction to go in.

And then today, I got a telegram. The boy who delivered it sped away on his bicycle like his life depended on it, despite the black ice.

Stan is dead. Or so they say. I refuse to believe it. I still fully expect him to walk in, large as life, say hello love, put the kettle on, there's a doll. I had an earlier dream, yesterday evening. I dreamed of him. I sat in my old rocker and closed my eyes, and I was with him. Young again, just the two of us holding hands up in Shrewsbury Park, love in his eyes for me, and me alone.

The telegram's made my mind up. We're going to Yorkshire. No more humming and hahing. I've got butterflies in my stomach. I've never been north of London since the day I set foot in this country. I wonder what they're like up in Yorkshire, and how long it takes to get there? All I've heard is that it's cold, dark, and hilly. I hope Stan will know where to find me, if he does make it home. If he's alive. But I have to go, I realise that now. I need to be among people who knew—know—him.

I can't write any more. I can't see the page and the ink is smudging.

1ˢᵗ *January 1941*

I'm trying to get everyone's names in my head and teach the children too, so they won't sound ignorant and can behave themselves and address everyone properly. There's Stan's uncle Harold. He fought in the last war and lost a leg, so he hobbles about with a wooden one. Obviously, couldn't fight in this war. Then there's his wife Margaret—I think they call her Maggie. And there's Betty or Bess, Maggie's sister who lives nearby. I get the feeling she spends a lot of time there. I don't think Betty or Bess (I'll have to ask her what she wants me to call her—I wouldn't want to get that wrong) ever married. I think she might have looked after their parents until they died, and now lives in the old family home. No doubt she rattles around in it. Anyhow, Harold and Maggie have two married sons whose families live not far away. Peter and his wife, Mary, and Stephen—they call him Steve, thankfully—who is married to someone called Iris. Of course, the men are off fighting. They've each got kids, but I haven't yet got them in my head. They (Harold and Maggie, that is) also have an unmarried daughter called Agnes, which could get tricky, though she's away in the land army. Maybe I'll revert to Frances while I'm up there. That shouldn't cause any confusion as Stan's sister Frances is a land girl down in Kent and so we won't be seeing her.

We'll be staying with Uncle Harold and Auntie Maggie, helping them out. They have a Victorian terrace big enough to take us all in. It's got three bedrooms apparently, only one of which they use, and a big attic where kids can bed down. Esther and I will share a bedroom in case they need the other one at any point. It makes for fewer bedrooms to heat. The baby will come in with us when it's born. There's a smallholding in their back garden leading down to the railway.

What if they don't like us, or the children get on their nerves? I hope mine can play with their cousins up there, and that they all get on. I guess they're second cousins, aren't they? And how will Esther manage, being in yet another new place? Oh well, time for bed. And bombs. Not for much longer though.

4ᵗʰ *January 1941*

Well, we're here in Keighley, in the West Riding of Yorkshire. It's so different from South-East London I feel like I'm in a foreign country. The accent's so hard to understand, it's like when I stumbled off the boat, as a little girl. The first thing I heard when I stepped down from the train (big drop by the way) was, "Now then!" It sounded like I was in trouble, though I've managed to glean that it basically means "Hello!"

All the walls of the houses and factories are blackened with soot—which makes me feel right down in the dumps. The fields, instead of being lined with hedges like in Kent, have these dry stone walls made of bits of stone piled on top of each other. They're black, too. As is the sky. Talk about black over Will's mother's. As I got out the train, the stench of muck spreading on the fields made me gag. Disgusting smell.

And it is so cold! I brought my mittens with me, but they're useless when I'm peeling veg. It's even harder to work myself up to going outside to the lav than at home, and here they have one of those old-fashioned wooden seats that goes right across the width of the privy, with a rusty old chain that doesn't always flush, so you have to pull it several times. The cistern, I'm told, is likely to freeze overnight too, so when I went this morning, it had someone else's business in there, plus newspaper of course as there is no such thing as toilet paper in this house. The lavatory is quite a way down the garden. You get to it by going downstairs from the living room and then into the cellar—which is damp, as the house is built into the hillside. On the ground floor, the kitchen has a lovely range that's always lit so they can put the kettle on or boil up a few bones to make broth. The heat rises, so one small blessing is that the bedroom Esther and I sleep in is lovely and warm, especially with the eiderdown they've given us. We have to share a double bed, but I don't mind. The boys, though, being right up in the attic, don't fare so well. They've got to sleep on rugs, and we left our rag rugs behind because we couldn't carry them. I was sad about that, especially having made them so recently, but needs must. I'll have to make more. They've only got a woollen blanket each and no sheets, so I've told them they can sleep in their school clothes and we'll wash them every week. They've got two pairs of shorts each, and two shirts but only one cardigan for each boy. The school uniform up here is a different colour, but I'm sure the headmistress won't mind so long as I send them looking smart. Mind you, they'll stick out like sore thumbs. Everyone will know they're evacuees. I just hope they don't get picked on. I know what it is, to be the odd one out, looking and sounding different from the other kids at school. But I hope they won't start talking Yorkshire.

It was a long journey—the longest I've done since I arrived in this country. We got up before the break of day and grabbed our things while the bombs were falling all around us, then caught the first bus to Woolwich Arsenal train station. The first train took us to Charing Cross where we got on a bus to Kings Cross. I had a look at the tube station, just out of curiosity. I've not been on a tube in ages, not since my single days. Each station is now home to several families, and many more overnight. They've set up in little corners, with their bedding and the odd photograph. It was hard, lugging suitcases on and off buses and trains in my condition. But Esther and the boys were absolute troopers. Everyone did their bit to make sure we caught the evacuation train. Once safely on it—if you can call it safely given Jerry's habit of gunning them—I gave the boys and Esther a sardine sandwich each and some water, and they all fell asleep, David stretched out across me while I sat by the window, Esther at the other side of David with her head on the wall, then the other two boys went head to toe opposite us. Another six kids were crammed into our carriage, sleeping where they could with their gas masks tied to little labels round their necks saying who they were and where they were going. Poor little mites. My heart went out to their mums as they hugged and kissed them goodbye. I'm sure many of the children thought they were going on a big adventure, laughing and joking and kicking each other, at least the boys were. Until it came time to say goodbye to their mothers. At one point, someone started singing, and before long the whole station was performing "Wish me luck as you wave me goodbye" and "Doing the Lambeth Walk." They even danced to that one. The moment when those mothers had to let go of their children was heart breaking, though. The women shoved their kids off, a smile pasted on their faces, giving last minute instructions like, "Look after your little sister," "Don't forget to wash behind your ears," and "Write home as soon as you get there to tell me all about it." As the children piled on the train, I could see those women looking so brave as they waved. Many were still waving their hankies as we turned the corner out of the station. A little bit of my heart broke off and flew towards them.

It took forever—literally all day—for our train to reach Leeds. We were constantly shunted into sidings so a train carrying troops or goods could pass. By the time we got there I was certain the family would have forgotten about us, and we still had two trains to catch. But miraculously, the Keighley train was in, and it wasn't long after that we made the relatively short journey on the branch line out to Damems. Several children from our carriage got off at various stops along the way to Leeds, others between Leeds and Keighley, all looking lost and sleepy. I hoped they would find kind families, not having to face what poor Esther went through. I shiver to think.

Anyway, despite us being so late, Uncle Harold and Auntie Margaret were there to meet us at Damems station. Auntie Margaret had a face like thunder, while Uncle Harold just looked anywhere but directly at us. I was determined to make the best of it. All smiles and plentiful thank you's despite wishing I could just sink into bed and cry myself to sleep.

Once we'd politely said hello and I'd introduced all the kids, making sure they remembered their manners, we struggled along the road to the house that will be our home for the foreseeable future. I've never been more grateful for a cup of tea and a slice of bread and butter in my life. I gave the boys a lick and a promise and sent them off to bed pretty sharpish, and Esther went off to our room. It occurred to me then, when I said we'd be sharing, she'd looked relieved rather than disappointed. The penny dropped as I saw her go up. She's safe with me. I'd defend her like I would one of my own.

Apart from the cold and the smell of manure, the other thing I noticed in the pitch black was the sound, or rather the lack of it. No bombs falling. I've got so used to the nightly bombardment it felt almost eerie not to hear it, or to see the night sky lit up. I never expected to feel like that. But I'll get used to it no doubt. And now, our new life begins.

6th January 1941

The children all start their new school today. I do hope they go on OK and can understand the other kids.

On our first night here, Margaret made a point of letting me know London isn't the only place that's been bombed. She keeps harping back to last August, when Bradford got it. One person died, but you'd think it was as bad as anything I've seen. I held my tongue, because I'm in her house. But I can see she and I won't see eye to eye on everything. It won't be like when I was in Ruth's house.

I think she thinks because I'm a Londoner I've got airs and graces. I put some lipstick on while I was on the train, because I wanted to look my best for them when they met us, but the first thing she said when she saw me, after "Now then!" was:

"You're all dolled up to the nines, aren't you lass?" — as she looked me up and down without a trace of a smile. She then went "humph" as she turned to lead the way to her house. She made no attempt to help carry, despite my delicate condition. Uncle Harold did, peg leg and all.

10th January 1941

The kids seem to have settled into their new school, Mama, even Esther, though it's hard to tell as she says so little. She's too polite, and I've got no energy to bring her out of her shell. Why on earth did I take on another child when I can hardly look after the ones I've got?

Aunt Margaret's sister, Bess, spends pretty well all day and every day round here, sitting in the best armchair, demanding cups of tea. She told me the day we arrived she's got blood pressure, and that's why she can't do much. If you ask me, she's a bit full of herself. Uncle Harold just grunts one-word answers when I ask him if he'd like a cuppa. Otherwise, it's as if I'm not here.

I plod on, doing what I must for the children, but I feel as if I'm in a dream, or rather a nightmare, hoping I'll wake up from it, back in London with no bombs, no war. Stan working all hours in the butchers' shop, telling the kids bedtime stories. It's Friday already, and I don't seem to have done anything all week.

I'm getting black looks from Auntie Margaret writing this, so I'd better pull my socks up and sweep the kitchen.

15ᵗʰ *January 1941*

When the children are at school, the washing up stares defiantly at me from the sink as Auntie Margaret darns socks in her armchair, and the shirts that need ironing sit, arms crossed, in a corner. I don't go out unless I have to, and then I never look at whoever's serving me in these strange new shops. Maggie must've been talking about us, because everyone speaks to me in gentle tones, and no one seems to be taking umbrage at how rude I know I'm being, not making conversation like I normally do. I'm like a ship without a Captain, rolling out to sea. I keep going over my past with Stan, willing myself to relive every moment and bottle it. But then I find myself thinking about the future I thought we had together when Mr. Hitler's finished doing his worst, and as I stand at the sink, hands scalding, I collapse in a hopeless heap. Those days will never be, now. But then, I find myself thinking what if they've got it wrong? What if he's still alive, somewhere? He was in trouble. Maybe he found a way out. Maybe he'll walk in that door any minute and shout, "Surprise!"

I remember the day Stan asked me to marry him. He got down on one knee in the park. People kept walking past and stopping, looking back over their shoulders. Some of the older women turned their heads, tucking their chins into their necks and raising their hands to their mouths so I couldn't see them smile. I felt on cloud nine when he put that ring on my finger. Of course, I hadn't got a clue what marriage entailed. I just knew it meant having a house of my own, being a Married Woman, bringing with it a status not afforded to spinsters. And children. I always wanted lots of children, even though I didn't know what it took to bring them into the world—nor how hard I would work, for little tyrants who don't work themselves and won't do for many years yet.

He told me that day, as he put his arm around me to lead me back home so we could break the news—he'd already, unbeknownst to me, asked my Dad's permission—he told me, he said:

"I will never leave you Frances." He used my proper English name for once, even though I was already Agnes to everyone by then, because I'd been stepping out with him for a year already and got on famously with his sister, who was already the Frances in his life.

I'll never leave you. But that was before this bloody war, wasn't it?

Mum and Dad were so happy for me. They got on well with Stan, and he was always kind and respectful. They weren't so keen on him being a butcher at first, but he used to bring them the odd pound of sausages on a Saturday. He never saw his kids starve, neither.

See? I'm already talking about him in the past tense. It ain't right, is it? I refuse to believe my Stan's dead, telegram or no telegram. It didn't say nothing about what happened. Not a clue. Here's what it said:

"We regret to inform you that your husband Able Seaman Stanley Cockroft has been killed."

Not missing in action believed killed, not killed in the line of duty. Just killed. It's that bit that made me feel uneasy.

What if he's hiding somewhere, from whoever framed him for that murder? I'm more convinced than ever he's been framed for a crime he didn't—couldn't—commit. What if he's on the run? I suspect he's unable to tell the truth about who did it—maybe because he doesn't know, or maybe because if he grasses, it means certain death from whoever committed this awful, vile act. No. I'm not taking this one lying down, even if I do feel as if I just want to climb into bed and never get out. I wonder how Mr. d'Souza got on? I'll have to write to Sandhya.

I'd better snap out of this and start doing some housework. Maggie's giving me that look again.

82

16th January 1941

A particularly cold night last night—well below freezing. I was glad of sleeping next to Esther. I swear icicles were forming on my eyelashes, though that's probably my imagination. The snow's particularly bad up here. Mind you, I'm one of those strange creatures that quite likes fresh snow. I don't like slush, but I do like the way the snow makes people's voices sound as if they were in the same room as you, the clean white look to everything and the crunching sound under my shoes. Plus, I'm a big kid when it comes to snowflakes. I love watching them as they fall out the sky like they have all the time in the world, and then catching them in my hand, making them disappear. Snow is such a rare delight—even if I do then have to put my shoes and stockings by the fire afterwards. I feel guilty for having these thoughts, so soon after the terrible news. I wish I could cuddle up to Stan, hold him and smooth his hair back from his forehead. If I could make it all right for him, I'm sure he knows I would. I'd move mountains if I could.

Esther still looks to be having bad pains in her tummy. I sometimes catch her out the corner of my eye when we're sitting together with Maggie and Harold of an evening, sewing and knitting, and I see her hand move down to her tummy, below her waist. It's worse when she's on her monthlies, but she seems to have pains at other times, too. Poor little love. I wish there was something I could do. Maybe I'll mention it in my next letter to Ruth. She seems to know all sorts.

18th January 1941

I've heard from Sandhya. Her letter must have crossed with mine. No joy. Mr. d'Souza didn't get anywhere with the Navy. They wouldn't let him anywhere near—which makes me suspicious. It was kind of him to do this much. I wrote back immediately and thanked him and Sandhya. I haven't told the kids yet, about their dad and why we left London in such a hurry, but I think Adam suspects something because he keeps looking at me, as if my face holds the answer to a sum he's trying to work out.

I know I'm right, about Stan not being guilty. I just have to prove it. It looks like I am going to have to figure out a way to move that massive mountain!

The baby kicked all the way home from the shops today. When I got indoors, Maggie and Harold were out at their daughter-in-law's. Not sure which one. Anyway, I put my feet up, shut my eyes, and before I knew it, I was off on my travels, going at such speed I felt sick and dizzy. This time, Mama, I didn't come to see you.

I'm on a ship. It's very dark, and I can see a man hiding in the shadows. I know I'm invisible to him, so I don't feel too afraid even though my heart is racing. I walk towards him. He's wearing a white shirt, sleeves rolled up, and a butcher's apron. I know, somehow, that it's Stan's apron, but it isn't Stan wearing it. The apron, and the knife he's holding, are covered in blood, as you might expect for a butcher's things. But there's a lot of it, and the man's lips are curled into a snarly smile that makes my skin feel like it did when I was a kid and fell into a nettle patch. I follow his eyes to where he's looking down at the floor. A man lies dead, an open wound in his chest. There's blood everywhere, seeping out onto the ship's boards. A knife lies beside the body.

The man in the shadows kneels down, takes the dead man's finger in his own hand, and dips it in some of the fresh blood. Then he uses the finger to draw something on the boards beside the body. My heart jumps into my throat as I see the letters S then T then A. Then the kneeling man drops the hand, stands up, and rips off the apron. His own clothes underneath are merely dirty, not a speck of blood. He walks quickly towards one of the cabins, clutching the bloodied apron and knife, and I follow to see him drop them on the floor, beside one of the bunks. A bunk in which I see Stan's back, his shoulders hunched and face to the wall.

I came to, and noticed the clock on the mantelpiece was already showing three o'clock. I had to put what I'd seen behind me and get ready for the kids to come home, hungry as wolves no doubt. But the pictures inside my head wouldn't leave me alone. I know when the time is right, I will have to clear Stan's name, dead or alive. I hope beyond hope he'll be alive to see it but having seen the menace on that man's face, I'm no longer so sure. My heart beats at the speed of knots at the thought, and my head keeps going like it used to feel after getting off the roundabout when the big boys made it go too fast.

20th January 1941

After all the snow of early January, it's been thawing recently. I knew we were in for rain.

It never came yesterday. Today, bloody washing day, it hasn't stopped raining all day. I've had to get the range made up to dry the washing, but of course coal is in short supply. I just hope we manage to make it last. All the bedrooms here smell damp and I can't get comfortable temperature-wise, despite working like a trooper. That usually keeps me warm enough even if my hands are in and out of water all day long. I hate that feeling on my hands at the end of the day on Mondays. Like I've rubbed them in grit.

I can't tell anyone about what I saw on the ship, least of all Maggie or Harold. I'll just sound like a lunatic bound for Bexley, or wherever it is they send people round here. I try to carry on as usual, but I keep finding I've forgotten to put salt in the potatoes, sugar with the peas, or peel the carrots, all of which bring scowls. You'd think I'd tried to poison them.

When I'm not doing housework, and even when I am, I seem to collapse into myself, sobs pushing through quietly from deep in my insides, like the geysers in the north I heard about but never saw.

22nd January 1941

Hilda's husband has been called up. We all knew it would happen sooner or later, but Hilda's situation is different. He won't be going to fight. He's a conscientious objector. I remember her saying:

"How could a Christian go killing people? It's murder. I could not do that, and neither could Paul. We believe in Peace, not war."

Then she told me something that made a shiver go up and down my spine:

"One of the members of our Meeting for Worship told me he was a conscientious objector in the First World War, but he was refused CO status and carted off to France. Some conscientious objectors were shot, not always officially of course, but you know how there are 'accidents' in war."

Yes, and maybe there are still "accidents" when someone takes a dislike to you.

I remember reading about a CO in the Kentish Independent. His name and photograph were there, for all to see. I heard the man talked about at the corner shop and saw him refused chocolate even though he had the necessary coupons and the correct change—tuppence ha'penny. It must have been extra hard for him. His father was well known in the area, a Major Frank Smith M.B.E., who fought in the South African War at the end of the last century, and then again in the Great War, so called. Apparently, if the gossips are to be believed, the Major tried to get him an easy, safe job in the Pay Corps, with him. But this geezer stood firm. I heard him say to the shopkeeper that if he has to go to war, he doesn't want anyone fiddling a nice safe job for him. He isn't objecting to his own life being in danger, he said. He feels it's his Christian duty to obey the Lord's commandments, including Thou Shalt Not Kill. The newspaper reported that he had to appear before a judge at a Tribunal, but he hadn't realised he needed references from anyone, so they adjourned his case. I bet the poor bloke had got himself all worked up for that court appearance. Now he has to go again, with references, to see if they'll record him as a CO and send him off to work in some kind of land job, in all probability. At least in this war, that's allowed, whereas in the last war they were more often shamed and shot.

It'll be interesting to see what happens to Hilda's husband, Paul. They're already involved in such a lot of peace work. To be honest, if I didn't have the children to look after, I wish I could do more. There's something called the Friends Ambulance Unit, which goes behind enemy lines to pick up the wounded. Hilda, her being better educated than me, helps out with their Home Service Section. She deals with the applications and is involved with organising the supplies to the continent as well as sending staff to hospitals here in England. In fact, I've seen FAU ambulances in the Blitz, taking people to hospital and administering first aid. Apparently, the famous Cadbury family of chocolate fame is involved. They're a Quaker family. How ironic that the nice Mr. Smith was refused chocolate in our own corner shop, for being a conchie.

26ᵗʰ January 1941

Some days, it feels like the "Maggie and family" show around here. The daughters-in-law both turn up, together with their badly-behaved brats. My children don't get on with them. They're sullen and rude. Iris, Steve's wife, has a girl aged twelve who sighs a lot, reads occasionally, and without any invitation the other day, soon after we arrived, grabbed my hair and proceeded to plait it, causing me to wince. Mary, Peter's wife, also has just one child, though she is pregnant. Her boy is such a handful. He runs around the place, treading on my knitting, and throwing paper aeroplanes with a very loud sound accompaniment. God alone knows how Uncle H stands for it, but then he usually has his head in a book or the paper.

I heard from Ruth, about what I should do for Esther's tummy pains. She asked me if I'd noticed anything unusual in her underwear when I get it for the wash, like a yellowish or brownish discharge. But assuming that isn't the case, and it isn't, she suggested I just bide my time. It's unlikely she's been damaged internally, Ruth said, but to keep an eye on it. In time, the hope is the pain will subside.

27th January 1941

Esther awoke last night with a nightmare. Of course, I was awake immediately. I heard her—like a puppy's pathetic little yelp. She tried to tell me she'd be fine (her English has come on in leaps and bounds since I sent her to school), but she was shaking, bless her, so I told her to cuddle up and put her head on my chest. I didn't ask her what it was all about. Didn't want to upset her, though some say it's better out than in. I'm beginning to wonder if she's had nightmares before, when she was all alone with no one to comfort her. I wouldn't be surprised with what she's been through. Maybe when we're peeling spuds or something, I'll ask her if she wants to tell me.

We've all had colds of late. The relentless chill in the air tells me more snow is on the way, too. It always panics me when one of the boys gets a fever, but you've just got to carry on, haven't you, Mama? I miss my friends and neighbours back home, where if I need anything, I can always tap on Maud's next door, and she'll do what she can to help. More than once, we've lent each other a cup of sugar. It seems that particular staple goes back and forth more often than the Woolwich Ferry. Maggie and Harold make me feel in the way, even though I do as much as I can to make their lives easier. It's not that they complain. It's more the silence from him, and the looks from her, like she's saying you can't get the staff these days.

When the sirens go, I still tense up. But everyone up here just goes about their business. They don't even break into a run. My kids are getting the mickey taken out of them for doing just that. But my children know what would have happened if we'd been in a playground in London during daylight hours and the sirens had gone. They'd have been machine gunned where they stood as some Jerry plane swooped out of the sky. You see, it's not just the bombs we fear. They still have to do blackout up here, of course, and the buses still only drive with just enough light to see where they're going. It's not pleasant being out in the streets after dark, here. At least at home you knew there were always people about. Here, you fear someone will jump out of the shadows. And I can see the hills looming up at me, like some great big giant waiting to pounce.

I heard from Ruth again. Her husband Nathan is now in the air force. I can just see him in uniform. A handsome man if ever I saw one—so dark, and tall. If I were not married to Stanley God help him, and if Ruth were not my friend and married to him, I confess I'd be smitten. Anyway, he's a spitfire pilot now. They're much needed. Dangerous job, especially for such a gentle man. He had twenty-four hours' leave during his training, because his mother, who escaped the pogroms, had just died aged seventy. She must have been quite old when she had him, unless he's maybe older than he looks. Perhaps Ruth married an older man. The Jews bury their dead within a day, which is a tall order at the moment—and he might have had a few beers at the wake, because he told Ruth no pilot ever goes up without being slightly drunk. That shocked her. But he said they're all shit scared. His words, apparently. They fear the shame of not being able to get up there more than they do death, but they need the beer to help them, and their C.O. willingly supplies it. There is never a day when they all come back. Poor sods. To read our newspapers, you'd think it was only Jerry that suffers casualties. And them being the enemy, that's alright. They seem to forget those German pilots are some mothers' sons.

28th January 1941

I asked Esther about her nightmare, and about her tummy pains while I was about it. I'm glad I did—even if it did bring on some nightmares of my own. I managed to corner her after school, on the pretext of needing some help to carry shopping, then I suggested we walk through the park. She just nodded her head, as if she knew.

I don't know how I kept back the tears when she told me about the day she said goodbye to her mum. It brought it all back for me, about the day I lost you, Mama. Like me, she wanted to cling on, but unlike me, she was old enough to know she must let go. She knew her mum was making sacrifices to send her away, and she didn't want to make it harder for her.

As you know, her first digs weren't the safe haven she'd been promised. On her very first day, the farmer brushed his hand over her breast through the thin cloth of her blouse, whispering in her ear about her being a big girl as he leaned round to show her how to milk the cows. Later the same day, he pushed her up against the cowshed wall and pressed himself against her, almost suffocating her as he shoved his tongue into her mouth. As she told me, she looked as if she might vomit. She seemed to be watching it all on a tiny cinema screen on the ground. I couldn't help looking round to make sure no one was listening. There was only an old lady in the distance, concentrating on every step.

It took just one more day before the pushing against the wall led to him unbuttoning his flies, lifting her dress and pulling her drawers down. The first time he tried, she felt his thing against her thigh, but he was interrupted by a tractor from a nearby farm entering his yard. He slapped her round the cheek and sent her on her way.

He was more careful after that. Next time, he chose an evening when his Missus was on her way to bed. He ordered Esther into the yard on the pretext of her needing to re-do a job, shouting that she hadn't done it right as he pushed her out the door. He followed her out "to make sure," then once he'd got her in the barn he threw her down in the hay. This time, he did his business in her, it hurt like hell, and she bled. He told her if she squealed to anyone, he'd say she'd led him on and was a hussy. Called her a dirty Jew.

All the time she's telling me this, her eyes are wide with terror. She held onto her stomach, leaning forward, her voice almost a whisper. Every now and then the words seemed to catch in the back of her throat, making her cough and retch. I sat her down on a bench, bent over beside her, one hand resting on hers, willing the nightmares to leave her.

After her period didn't come, she was terrified. He watched her like a hawk, and when he realised she wasn't soiling any rags he told the Quaker woman who'd placed her that she was useless, and he wanted her gone. When she arrived, the Quaker insisted on speaking to Esther alone, despite protests and name-calling from the farmer. Esther told her she wanted to leave. She didn't mention her monthlies not coming, but she did say the farmer was brutal.

I asked her if he'd done anything to bring on the miscarriage, like poking anything other than his willy into her. Thankfully, the answer's no.

I hugged her, stroked her hair, and told her she's safe now. She kept sobbing, saying she's damaged goods, dirty. But I kept stroking her and telling her she's a pure child of God. I hope that made sense, because I meant it with all my heart.

6th February 1941

I got a letter from Stan today, dated some weeks ago. It came hand delivered by a man on crutches, with one leg. He said his name's George and he served with Stan. Lost his leg when a U-boat got their ship. Most of them managed to get into lifeboats and were picked up by the merchant navy. George figures he's lucky to be alive. Stan gave him this letter sealed in a tobacco tin a few days before the attack. He asked him if he ever got back to England to find me. George said you don't ever refuse that kind of request from a mate, because you never know when the grim reaper is going to come knocking. Of course, I was desperate to know whether Stan's alive or not, but he couldn't tell me. He just said as far as he knew they all managed to board the merchant navy ship, but because of his injury, this George was shipped home. It just so happens he lives in Bradford. He found me by contacting the welfare.

The letter's very odd. I'm copying it out here Mama, just in case I ever lose the original. Times are such you never know whether what you've got today, you'll have tomorrow. I sat reading it, holding in the other hand the neatly folded photograph I'd given him, of the two of us on our wedding day. Of course, Maggie was all eager to know what it said, as was Harold, but I wasn't going to read it out loud. It's my letter.

> *My darling Frances,*
>
> *If you are reading this, I am most probably dead. I've given this to my good friend George. He is as honest as the day is long, and I would trust him with my life. I have told him it would be better for him that he never knows the contents of this letter and he has taken me at my word. I have also sealed it in two envelopes, then put it in a tobacco*

tin and sealed the edges of that with animal fat in case it ends up in the water. I asked George, who does not himself smoke, if he would mind carrying it together with my photograph of us on our wedding day (which is also in said tin) in his breast pocket. He has willingly done so. We do things for each other when we can, especially when it comes to contacting each other's loved ones.

What I am about to tell you may shock you, but I know you will believe me because you know me to be an honest fellow. I have never lied to you, Agnes, in all the years I have known you. Sorry. I can never decide which of your names to use when I am writing. I'm using the one I have called you each and every day of our marriage. Aggie. My darling, headstrong, loving Aggie.

There is a man on this ship, the head cook. Name of Jim. He is a bad man, Ags. I have heard him talk with venom about other men on this ship. His face goes wild when he does, as if he has a demon in him. I've literally seen him foam at the mouth and spit as he speaks about people he doesn't like—which is anyone who gets in his way, it seems. He's a big man, too—bit of a belly but muscles to scare the bravest of men. I could easily imagine him picking up a fellow and swinging him above his head.

Anyway, this Jim had it in for a young lad called Pete, a rating like me who was a bit slow, bless him. I took Pete under my wing when he came aboard ship. He was assigned to kitchen duties but was only capable really of washing up and at that not terribly well. I covered for him because the cook would have held him up against the ship's wall and strangled him. I've seen him get hold of other, bigger men and the look of fear in their eyes was terrible. One man wet himself, which made Jim laugh and drop him, before kicking him in a very sensitive part of a man's body.

I was in my bunk (we're on shifts, of course — one in, one out so the bunk is used pretty well around the clock) when Pete dropped a tray of salt beef. Jim went spare. He strode out of the galley, but as he did so he grabbed my butcher's apron. He also had one of my meat chopping knives in his hand, recently sharpened by me.

I confess I stayed in my bunk, petrified, listening to the sounds of Pete pleading for his life, then several thuds, the last I guessed being the sound of him hitting the floor. I kept my eyes shut as I heard Jim creep back into my cabin, drop what I guessed was my knife and then I heard something softer fall to the floor, which I supposed was my apron, before he swiftly exited.

Before I could work out what to do next, as I stood pulling on my uniform, the captain came in and found my butcher's apron covered in blood, crumpled on the floor beside my bunk, and the very bloodied knife. Pete's body had a message written beside it in his own blood. It was the first three letters of my name — "STA." I'm sure I don't have to tell you they didn't need much more proof to pin the murder on me.

When they tried me, Jim waited outside, listening to proceedings. I wanted to open my mouth and tell the Captain about the way Jim had it in for the boy. I knew I was a goner whatever happened — either the Captain would shoot me himself, or Jim would be after me. But sense prevailed. I knew the death would be far worse if Jim got me, and if I snitched, he wouldn't give up until he did. A shot to the head is much cleaner. But then, there was a chance—a slim chance—that I might not get shot. But I am, as you know, an honest man. I could not tell an outright lie and say I had done it. So, I pleaded not guilty.

When it came to it, I decided not to dob Jim in it unless asked a direct question. None came. No-one wanted to hear what my thoughts were about who had carried out this foul murder, because they were all convinced it was me. And so, I stood in the dock for about an hour, maybe less, though it felt like an eternity, to my shame shaking like a baby, while they went through the evidence and came to their conclusion.

As you can imagine, I was convicted of the murder, and I was granted one last wish which, as you might guess by now, was to write this letter and give it to my mate. It has not been censored, because I told them I was writing down where to find you and other living relatives after the war has ended and enclosing a photograph of you so that he could be sure he found the right person. I wrote at breakneck speed, so apologies if the writing is bad.

And so, short of our ship going down tonight, I die at dawn tomorrow my love. Please know that I have loved you with all my heart. You are my precious jewel. I have never been unfaithful to you, neither have I been tempted. You have been a perfect wife and mother, for which I am eternally grateful.

My undying love,
Stanley

I checked with George. The U-boat struck that night. The ship went down. I couldn't keep that from Harold or Maggie. When Uncle heard, he dropped his newspaper and sat with his mouth open, his fag burning his fingers.

7ᵗʰ February 1941

So, is my Stan alive or dead? Did he have a premonition about the U-boat striking? If he made it onto the ship George was picked up by, did the other bloke—Jim—get there too, seek him out and kill him? Or did my husband face the Captain's bullet? I wish I knew the answers. It's killing me, not knowing.

But one thing's sure. I'm not batty. I did see what happened. Stan's account confirms what I saw on my travels. But I can't ever tell anyone. They would lock me up like a shot.

I knew a spiritualist once. They're making a comeback right now. There are some proper charlatans who know they can make a quick bob or two by plucking a popular name like Tom out of the air, saying they've got a Tom from the other side, in uniform. Load of made-up mumbo jumbo. But this woman I knew seemed genuine. She attended the spiritualist church long before the war started, and she told me there's this thing called astral travel where you go off visiting places in your astral body. I wonder if that's what happens to me? Except I don't just travel across space, but time too it seems. Sometimes when I travel, I go into a dream-like state, but I'm awake. Other times, my physical body is asleep, but my other body—my travelling, astral body—is never more alive, the colours never more vivid, the focus never sharper. It's as if I have special spectacles that make everything, including thoughts and sensations, as clear as my windows on a sunny day.

If I saw what happened on that ship, maybe I did also meet one of my kin through the radio. And I'm certain I do see you, Mama.

But how in heaven's name am I going to clear Stan's name?

99

15th February 1941

Today, I heard from Ruth, which provided some relief from my torment. She, Hilda, and Sandhya still stand down in Beresford Square as often as they dare, holding placards for the Peace Pledge Union. The No More War lot, who joined forces with the PPU, got really big after the last war. Ordinary people had a lot of sympathy with them, but of course now they get spat on and called names that would have my mum turning in her grave, all because they stand up for peace. Mind you, the PPU isn't asking for actual peace anymore, just support for conscientious objectors.

Most people think the PPU don't have any respect for the men who are fighting for our country, but they've got the wrong end of the stick. I didn't get it myself at first, but I'm slowly coming round to understanding why they demonstrate. I suppose I see myself as one of them now, even if I do still feel a bit wobbly about it. The Peace Pledge Union simply think war is a bad idea. If you count the dead, both civilian and service personnel, surely anyone in their right mind would agree? That's not saying we don't respect and honour our men. The opposite! We want them home in one piece! I was always taught by Mum and Dad that you can't beat violence with violence. Only love will prevail over hate. What they said makes more and more sense now. And Hilda's taught me that the Germans are just like us. They aren't monsters. They're just having their heads filled with Nazi claptrap. Even over there, some people resist the Nazis and are getting shot for it! We don't hear about them or think about how their lives are controlled by the Nazis. We're taught to hate all Germans. Some German people are risking their necks to protect their Jewish neighbours—people they grew up with, played with, went to school with, worked with, fell in love with. It doesn't bear thinking about. I got quite fond of Ruth's kids, not to mention Esther now of course. I couldn't bear the thought someone would harm those poor Jewish children. Apparently, Hitler's got it in for people who are lame or slow, too, not to mention Gypsies, communists and homosexuals. But if we support war, we support the very mentality that leads to deciding who should live and who should die, when we're all God's children. It's hatred we need to fight, not each other. I'm no expert, mind. I haven't got a clue how to argue with hecklers. So, it's just as well I'm not standing there, holding up placards.

Ruth told me this woman came up to them, three kids in tow. She was carrying one small child in her arms and holding on like a vice to her second youngest's wrist. She looked as if she might break it, the poor kid. The oldest child had big, staring eyes and his little body was cowed over, like he expected to be beaten at any moment. They all looked as if they could do with a good wash, her included. Anyway, she ran up rather than walked, then stood right in front of Hilda and spat in her face.

She then proceeded to shout abuse, along the lines of:

"Bunch of traitors! How dare you stand in your best Sunday clothes, preaching peace? Don't you know our men are fighting for you? Do you want to be speaking German in a year's time, and have your children brought up speaking German?"

And so on.

Ruth replied to her in Yiddish. The woman must have thought it was German. She handed the baby to the oldest child who looked weighed down but obediently did as he had to, and she let go of the other child's wrist—then she flew at Ruth. The women—there were about six in all—surrounded Ruth. Sandhya called out, "She's Jewish!" but another woman said, "That's not the point." Anyroad, they stood firm, linking arms, Hilda with spit still dripping down her face. Eventually, the woman grabbed both of the smaller children and stormed off.

Poor Ruth. After telling me all that, she dropped in that her husband Nathan, the one I told you about who's so lovely and gentle and was called up to fight in the RAF, has been shot down. He's now a POW behind enemy lines in France.

22ⁿᵈ February 1941

It's so hard to concentrate at the moment, what with the cold, the heartburn and breathlessness, the worry about Stan, and having still to do such a lot around the place. I'm around seven months gone now and look like the side of a house.

Still, there are moments. Moments of relief, when I can forget I'm away from home, there's a war on, and my man isn't here. Today, it was snowing hard, and some boys came to call for my three. They had some tea trays with them, and said there's a good hill nearby, where they all go when it snows, so I wrapped them up as best I could and sent them packing. They came back, all smiles, ruddy cheeks, wet through, and saying they were starving and freezing of course. I made them go upstairs and change and rub themselves with a towel. When they came down, I made them a cup of hot tea each, and a lunch of toast and dripping, which they wolfed down. They'd been out about three hours!

1st March 1941

More colds. It's that time of year, I suppose. Adam, who is usually very hardy, has developed a nasty cough. I made them all do salt gargles when they told me they had sore throats. Uncle Harold joined in for good measure, so it was a proper din, but it might have helped. I'm keeping Adam off school, so I can keep an eye on him. He's burning up, and I don't have to tell you, Mama, it scares me witless to see him like that.

I've got him inhaling Friar's Balsam as I write this, and I'm making a cough medicine from some cut up onion on a saucer with a tiny bit of sugar. It'll make a syrup, and I'll spoon that into him four times a day. I'm also grabbing whatever I can to prop him up in bed, so it doesn't get a hold on his chest. I'm praying, fiercely.

6th March 1941

Well, I don't know whether it was the onion syrup, the inhaling, the propping up or the prayers, but thank God Adam seems a lot better, and touch wood for now we're all germ free.

I'm sending him back to school tomorrow, Friday or no Friday. He's missed enough schooling, and besides, I've had enough of him being under my feet, moping around.

10th March 1941

I'm glad I sent Adam back to school. He seems completely recovered, and today the boys' new friends all called for them again. They don't seem to care that David is little. They pat him on the head, and smile, and he loves it.

They know a place where people dump the things that can't be repaired, and they've found some old pram wheels there. They've taken apart an old broken drawer, and made a seat so, with some old odd bits of rope tied together they've made a kind of cart. They pull David along on it, which he loves, but when they get to the hill (where the snow has now gone, at least for now) they go haring down there, hell for leather.

Yesterday, they made a den in the woods, using yet more stuff they have scavenged. I think the boys are having a great time, to be honest. It's amazing how they adapt—far better than us adults.

13th March 1941

I've got a thing about rats and mice, especially rats. It's the stories I've heard about how, if you corner them, they'll try and jump over your shoulder, but in the process, they'll go for your throat. And they're so big. I remember when I was a little girl hearing scratching in the corner of my bedroom at night, lying there sweating and waiting, convinced at any moment one would make its way into my room and attack me, and no one would know as I lay there dying. Haha! I've always had an active imagination!

Well, last night I didn't even hear any scratching. I was fast asleep, curled up round Esther, when I reached up to my head and as I woke, I knew I was trying to scratch an itch. Except it was more than an itch. I could feel the claws, ever so light in my hair as it moved across my head and face. I screamed before I could think about waking the house up. The thing scuttled off me, and I lay there for a long time after that, my heart playing a military drum in my ears. I had to get up to use the potty after a bit, of course. I felt around the edges and onto the floorboards first, to make sure I wasn't going to have any claws you-know-where.

I got up this morning to hear Aunt Maggie clattering around below. When I sheepishly came downstairs in my nightgown, she looked daggers at me for being so lazy, so I apologised (I never forget my manners, Mama) and said I hadn't had much sleep because something had crawled through my hair in the night. I also apologized just in case I'd woken her with my shameful screaming.

"Eee!" She says, looking all superior like, as if she's enjoying this moment of my humiliation. "That'll be a field mouse. You mustn't mind them, lass. I'm surprised you haven't seen one before now. That's what you get if you live near fields. You'd best get used to it, 'cos there'll be more, make no mistake."

I wish they'd get a cat. If only I'd let the kids bring one of the ones that had been bombed out they kept bringing to me, hoping I'd want another small mouth to feed.

I think I felt a twinge just now. That shock hadn't better have brought on the labour. I'm not due for a while, yet.

16th March 1941

Well, I have a daughter, born March 14th, 1941!

Labour did indeed start after that shock. By the evening, I was in strong labour and the midwife was sent for. She attended me in my own bedroom, so I can lie in here. We've got a makeshift crib. Auntie Maggie and Uncle Harold have several large oak chests of drawers with lovely tongue and groove joints. Nice and sturdy. I have one in my bedroom, and luckily, I'd already cleared a drawer to put by my bed. I'd also managed to bring a few bits of bedding from London, along with terry nappies and such like. And I had a matinee coat that I knitted in the evenings after the kids were in bed, and a bonnet and mittens.

The birth itself wasn't too bad, what with having had four already. It was over by four o'clock the next morning. The midwife was stern but good at her job and left me nice and clean with my little one already latched on.

My daughter (it sounds so funny, writing that) is a greedy little thing, and as a result, I'm a bit sore. She looks like one who knows what she wants out of life and is determined to get it—not like her Mama, who before the war wouldn't have said boo to a goose. Funny how wartime changes you. I've got opinions now. I've got Hilda to thank for that. Mind you, Auntie Margaret still scares me, as does her sister.

Having a girl born premature, such a precious little thing, has made me so afraid that she'll be taken from me, just like my darling Stephen, God rest his soul. Dare I love her?

I look at her, and I see her stunningly blue eyes, unlike my own, but then of course she's not the first of my babies to have Stan's blue eyes. Her reddish skin, pale underneath. It's almost like she's not really mine, just lent to me for a little while. I wonder, will we be the best of friends? Or will she hate me for being so dark? Or for not being neat like some other children's mothers? Will she like jellied eels, or Yorkshire pudding? What books will she fall in love with? Will she also finger the shiny, delicate pictures in *What Katy Did*, or will there be other books for her to fall into, like warm snug caverns that no one else is allowed in?

And will she use her vote? Will she understand what it took to get it? Of course, I didn't personally contribute to ensuring she and other girls like her will have that particular right. I was too young, but I knew of women who did, and they were brave women, all of them. Some were chucked out by their husbands for bringing shame on the family, slung in the clink for standing up for what they believed to be right. Some lost their kids. Many were spat on, not just by men but by women too, who, for some reason, thought it was shameful to want the right to vote for proper representation. Some suffragettes were maltreated by the police who arrested them. And of course, Emily Davison lost her life under the King's horse. I only know that because my mum talked about it; it happened before I was brought to England. Of course, when some women did get the vote in 1918 along with all men, that wasn't the end of it. It was criminal that working-class women who weren't yet thirty or didn't own any property were still denied that right. When all women over 21 got the vote in 1928 I was still too young, but as soon as I was old enough, I voted. And I have exercised that right ever since.

I must be more political than I give myself credit for, because I'd defend it with all I've got, that right for ordinary working-class women to vote, just as I'd defend the working man's right to a good decent job with fair wages and fair breaks. And of late, I think I'd fight for peace, too, wherever I can—though I suspect that view would not be popular round here. I miss my friends Hilda, Sandhya and Ruth. I must write them a collective letter.

I'm wondering how long Aunt Maggie will allow me to lie in. The midwife says two to three weeks, but I bet Auntie will want me up in about ten days to help with all the chores she's suddenly presented with. Esther will be helping—I know. She's a good girl. But Aunt Maggie will expect me to show my face soon, you can be sure.

I've decided to call the baby Susan. It's a modern name, and to my way of thinking it spells hope. When the midwife asked me what I would call her, I felt guilty. I should be consulting Stan on this, but she needs a name. I felt this great gaping hole, though, in my chest. He isn't here to share in my joy. He doesn't even know he's got a daughter. Just what he hoped for.

18ᵗʰ *March 1941*

Uncle Harold surprised me by popping upstairs to see the baby today. I asked him about the mills here, and how they're used in the war effort. Apparently, they spin khaki. It's important war work, and since I asked, Aunt Maggie tells me so at every opportunity, her chin pulled in and her lips downturned as she grabs her bosom and hauls it up. I wonder if I'll ever get her approval?

Listening to the radio, it seems Lord Haw-Haw has been here. He knows about the mills spinning khaki. Is there anywhere he doesn't know about? I can hear Bess downstairs while I lie here, making loud comments she knows I can hear, about "them Londoners" and "them snooty-nosed Southerners," usually when reading out something to Maggie, from Uncle Harold's newspaper. Now, I've noticed he's very particular about the way he folds his newspaper. Always leaves it with a nice, neat crease, and all the pages in order. But when she gets hold of it she pretty well demolishes it. I did take to folding it after she leaves and replacing it by his chair in a quiet act of solidarity with the old fella. But of course, while I'm lying in, it'll be its own paper version of a bomb site.

What with Bess, and the daughters-in-law, plus their brats, I'm glad to be upstairs, though I know when they've appeared, as the noise carries.

There's an isolation hospital here in Keighley. It's for diphtheria and scarlet fever. I hope none of mine ever needs it because you can't visit them there for a whole month. I hate to think of those children, all alone without their parents to hug them to sleep at night. It makes me think of our Stephen. And Esther. And if I'm honest of me, when I was little. But I don't want to dwell on that, Mama.

I worry about Esther. Aunt Maggie has her looking after me and the baby, which is fair enough, though that in itself is a lot. She has to empty my po, and I've got a metal bucket in the corner of the room where I throw all the nappies and my rags when they get too sopping wet. She has to boil all that lot up on the stove and try to get them dry on the guard round the range. On Mondays, though of course, Maggie's washing takes precedence and so I sometimes have to put wet rags in my knickers and damp nappies on the baby. Then we just huddle together, and I hope we can keep each other warm. Esther also dusts and sweeps my room and does the normal washing when she can. I only have two nightgowns for Susan, so I sometimes just let her lie in it if it's not soiled, just wet. She dries out in bed with me. When it comes to changing bed sheets, we top and tail. They only get washed every other week. I'm dying for a bath, but I'll have to do that when Uncle Harold is out, which isn't very often. He does a lot of sitting around and reading the newspaper, expecting cups of tea and his meals. He's nice enough, don't get me wrong—they both are I suppose, even though Aunt Maggie lets you know whose house it is. That's the thing. I do feel like we're in the way.

Esther has to run errands for Aunt Mags, like going to the corner shop for supplies. Auntie tries to avoid the heavy work, which I can't blame her for. She must be pushing sixty. You'd think she'd be delighted to have Esther—all that extra help. But it doesn't seem that way.

I'll have to get up after ten days. I'll be ready for it by then anyway.

20ᵗʰ March 1941

It's Henry's tenth birthday today, and I've had no chance to do anything for him, laid up here with a new baby. I'll have to find a way to make it up to him next year. I must ask Auntie Margaret if she has any rags she'd like me to make into rag rugs for her, while I'm making them for the children. Maybe that'll get her on side.

I've had a letter from my brother David all the way down south in Kent. I felt guilty when I spotted his handwriting. He doesn't know he's got a niece yet—I've been too busy and tired to write and tell him. I held the envelope for a while before opening it, feeling its shiny paper and turning it over in my hands, looking at the postmark, which gave it away of course.

It made me homesick reading it, even though we didn't see all that much of each other what with him living in Whitstable and me in Plumstead. It's a long and complicated train journey, and very expensive. In fact, before the war broke out, no one would have thought of upping sticks and travelling as far as I have with these children.

I remember you telling me that, once upon a time, the town where we lived was full of adventurers and gold miners (though many had left by the time I was born, the gold and their luck having run out). Some of them had come a long way—like from China. It's different here, in England. I occasionally see brown or olive-skinned people, like Sandhya and Ruth, and when I do it makes me feel less like I stick out like a sore thumb. But when I was growing up in South-East London, that's exactly how I felt. If I'd been across the river, where the Jews lived in the East End, I might not have felt so out of place, because many of them are darker skinned. Now, my boys stand out here in Yorkshire, because of their southern accents and their strange school uniforms.

My brother David may not be my blood, but he is my kin. I'm sure you would understand that, Mama. In our own extended family, I have some vague memory of foster children. Family is more than blood, and he's always called me his little skin and blister, which when we were kids made me feel special. Still does. We always had a bond, despite not looking the slightest bit like each other.

And here I am, raising Esther just as Mum and Dad did me. They may have been wrong to adopt me, taking me far away from my own land, but I see now they thought they were doing the right thing, and they treated me just as well as they did their own blood-child. I grew to love them. I've only properly realised all of this since losing them. Perhaps I feel looking after Esther is payback for their love, I don't know. Anyhow, I just feel it's right.

Mum and Dad brought us both up to be good God-fearing folk, and although I don't get to church these days except on high days and holidays, I pray to the Christian and Jewish God, and to Jesus—but I'm also close to the land, Mama. I sometimes think, when I'm outdoors here in England, if only I could travel through the centre of the earth to you, I would be home. When I go on my travels, that's exactly what it feels like. Knowing all of this means I'm always home—just the other side of the door from you, Mama. I haven't had the energy to visit you of late, so for now that thought will have to do.

David's letter was very short. He's a man of few words. But I read it several times while I was feeding Susan this morning. Esther brought the letter to me. Aunt Maggie hasn't been near apart from visiting soon after the birth, to make sure she didn't have a monster in her midst. You'd think she'd take *some* interest in her great-niece.

Here's what he said:

Dear sister,

I heard you had gone north to your husband's family. That is a good decision. You need to put the safety of those children first, above all else.

I was sorry to hear the news about Stan. Yours is a tale so familiar these days. When this war is over, there will be many widows left. God alone knows how we will rebuild this country.

I am busy farming here in Whitstable. Every spare inch of land, no matter how sandy the soil, is being used. Of course, it's not my land, but I am working it and getting a wage for it, so I can't grumble. I'd rather be flying spitfires or Lancasters, but they won't let me with my poor eyes, whereas I can make myself useful here.

Brenda sends her love.

David and Brenda

Like I say, short and sweet. But at least he bothered to write. It brought home to me that I might have to accept what they say, that Stan is dead. It seems everyone else thinks he is.

21st March 1941

In the second post came a letter informing me that I won't receive any more of Stan's pay. It was delayed. In fact, I haven't had anything all year so far, not since the beginning of January. As far as they're concerned, he *is* dead, and that's that. Of course, Bess had to comment when I popped downstairs for a cup of tea.

"What did you expect?"

I could see the corners of her mouth turning down, like she was talking to a troublesome girl who's no better than she should be. I suppose that's exactly what I am, to her. I come here with my kids in tow, and what does she know of me?

I'll get a widow's pension—or at least I hope I will. It depends on whether they think he died in action, serving his country—or whether the fact that he was convicted of murder just before the U-boat hit means I'm now destitute! I can't bear to think about that, but clearly, I'll have to do something to make sure I can put bread on the table for all these children. Of course, if I can clear his name … Oh my God, my head's like jelly. Now there's something I haven't seen in a while. Jelly. How can I be thinking of jelly, at a time like this?

24ᵗʰ March 1941

I got up and went to church today, Mama, exactly ten days after giving birth to Susan. Aunt Margaret said I should to give thanks for a safe delivery. I got the impression she and Bess also think I'm not clean enough to have in her house until I've been churched. Well, now I am. I'm certain she also wanted to get me out of bed and back to pulling my weight. I shouldn't have gone downstairs the other day. My legs feel as if I've been at sea for a month, but now I'm up I'll just have to keep going and get stronger.

Auntie Margaret is also trying to persuade me to let the mortgage company know about Stan's death. Payments were coming out of his pay, and as you know, Mama, that's been stopped. It's the last thing I want to be doing right now, when I am up half the night and can't see straight, but I suppose she's right.

One good thing—on my way back from the church I bumped into a woman I didn't know from Eve. They all know each other's business round here, and so she knew who I was. She said she's got some children's things at home that she's been hanging onto, waiting for one of hers to produce a grandchild, but now the boys are all away she says she might as well give the clothes to me.

"I daresay you can make use of un," she barked, in that Yorkshire way, without so much as a smile. I shall have to get used to that, I suppose, along with the blackened stone that still makes me want to cry.

I shall take a good look through the clothes when they come, and if there's anything that's useless for the baby I'll use it to start making my rag rugs.

30ᵗʰ March 1941

It's hard to find time to write to you now, Mama. I spend my days working so hard. I never stop. Susan wakes at regular intervals all night long, and I get up to get the children ready for school around seven so I can get the nappies on to boil first. Aunt Maggie doesn't expect me to do full duties yet, but I have to muck in where I can. Of course, whenever I think I've got things under control, Susan wakes and screams her head off until I feed her. Aunt Maggie thinks I'm too soft on her and should show her who's boss. She says I'm making a rod for my own back. But I hear the poor little mite cry, and my milk lets down, and so it's either feed her or be wet through. I can't stand to hear her cry. It tears me apart.

That lady from down the road came round with a great big bag of children's clothes and emptied them out on the floor of the living room. I could see Mary looking them over, but this lady—Mrs. Wright, her name is—told her in that typically forthright Yorkshire way:

"Now, don't you be getting any designs on this lot, lass. This is for our evacuee. She hasn't much to her name, having had to travel so far with all these little'uns, and in her condition at the time. You've got your family around you. This lot's for her."

Mary silently got up and filled the kettle, put it on the range, looked out the window as if checking whether it might rain, then took up her knitting.

I've come up to my bedroom early now the nights are getting a little lighter. I can see to write without having to light more than one candle beside the bed. Susan is sleeping peacefully, and the boys are all safely snoring above us. I don't seem to have the time or energy to go on my travels these days, much like writing really. I'm starting to make the rag rugs, though. When I told Auntie Margaret of my plans, she said she could do with a new rag rug to put in the privy and one by the front door. I said that's a good idea, but can she give me any rags she doesn't want? She found a pair of old trousers that wouldn't do as cleaning rags. It's a start.

But all is not well. I have no widow's pension, and I'm beginning to think I probably won't get one, no seaman's pay, and so no money at all. I'm completely reliant on Aunt Maggie and Uncle Harold's charity. Plus, I suspect rumours will have got out that I'm the wife of a murderer who killed a fellow sailor at sea. That Bess won't be able to keep her trap shut. I know it's a lie, but they don't.

I've got to do what I can to clear his name, Mama. I'll start by writing to that fellow who came to tell me—Lieutenant Arthur Wright. Thinking about it, he didn't have to come and see me in person. I think he was trying to tell me he believed my husband to be innocent, but the evidence was stacked against him. Maybe he can help. And I'll ask Sandhya again. She must have learned something from her husband over the years. I may be clutching at straws but it's time to get writing, and not this diary! Time's too precious. In the meantime, I need to earn a living so that I can pay my way here.

1st April 1941

I've wasted no time, Mama. I've written to that Lieutenant and asked him if there's any way he can help. It wasn't an easy letter to write. I don't really have a clue what his opinion is of my husband, and I fear I might not have given him a very good impression of myself. I don't know what he can do, if anything, and I suspect I might be whistling in the dark—but I have to try.

I also wrote to Sandhya, but with no expectation of anything she can actually do to help.

April Fools' Day today. Let's hope the joke's not on me.

6th April 1941

Isn't it funny, Mama—or strange, perhaps, not funny—that even when there are truly awful things happening you can still find some comfort in nature? Today, I took the kids down to the park and there were some horse chestnut trees in bud. When I was a kid we always called them sticky buds. And you know what? I had to touch them. I think I'm the biggest kid of all! If we're still here in the autumn, we can go searching for conkers—and if not, we can do it in Shrewsbury Park back home. Adam already knows how to toughen them up in vinegar, and last year he learned to make a hole with one of my knitting needles and thread string through, tying a good knot at one end. He had a really good conker last year—a tenner!

It's an innocent enough game, is conker fighting. No one gets hurt. Just a few conkers splattered about the garden. Maybe that's one thing he can play with Mary's boy. If we're still here.

Anyway, I did as Auntie Margaret suggested and let the mortgage company know my husband is deceased. I had to send them a copy of the death certificate, having first got hold of that. It's all a big palaver. But Mama, one very good bit of news is, Stan's death means not only that I no longer have to make the mortgage payments, but the mortgage is now paid off! We never discussed that sort of thing, but I suppose he must have set it up that way when he took out the mortgage. I own a house! I still have no actual money, but I do have a house. It feels strange, to be a property owner in my own right. I never thought about it while Stan was alive. It was all in his name, him being the man. But now, I am a woman of means. Well, maybe not means, but a woman of property. It sounds very grand.

What's more, Mrs. Wright paid another visit today. Apparently, she's been all round the congregation in her church, asking for donations for "our evacuees." She came with her arms full of clothes, including precious coats and some shoes. It brought tears to my eyes. I could hardly believe people's generosity. I didn't know what to do with myself, standing there holding a beautiful silk dress someone had decided was no longer needed. It's apple green, my favourite colour, and it'll fit me a dream, once I've lost a bit of my baby tummy. I really wasn't expecting anything for myself. I told her so, as I handed her a cup of tea. She shrugged, sniffed, and said:

"Folk do what folk do. I'm only the messenger."

Which I knew was not entirely true.

10ᵗʰ *April 1941*

I got a response from Sandhya today, bless her. She must be worried sick about her hubby, but she still took the time to reply to my letter. She can't offer any real advice though, Mama, just encouraged me not to give up.

Nothing yet from the Lieutenant.

12ᵗʰ April 1941

Adam is eleven years old today, Mama! Your oldest grandson, in all probability. I managed to make a card by cutting a picture of a motor car out of a newspaper and sticking it onto an old card Aunt Maggie gave me, using a bit of flour and water for the glue. He looked pleased enough. He's a good kid. He knows if I could have done more for his birthday I would have. Gave me a big hug and told me I'm the best Mum in the world. I didn't know where to put myself, so I just called him a daft ha'p'orth and pushed him away. Now, of course, I wish I hadn't.

I also got a snooty letter from the Lieutenant, very formal, just telling me that due process would be followed. I'm at a dead end.

13th April 1941

I went to church today, Mama. It happens to be Easter Sunday, which is a much happier day than Good Friday I've always thought. I can't be doing with all that dying on the cross business. Life's terrifying enough as it is, without thinking about Jesus hanging there in pain and suffering, making us feel guilty for it with all that talk of him needing to do it to save us from our own sins.

Anyway, I thought, if man has failed me in my efforts to clear Stan's name, maybe God can help. I don't know if I was imagining it, but I felt people were staring at me as I queued up to take Holy Communion, with Susan in my arms. The priest was lovely, though. He shook my hand just like everyone else's at the end of the service. In fact, he seemed to hold onto it a bit longer than everyone else's. If I wasn't so dog tired and rushed off my feet, I might go again and sod the busy bodies. Forgive my swearing, Mama.

14th April 1941

I managed finally to get Susan's birth registered. I think I'd been putting it off, hoping to have a husband to do it for me like he did with the others. He was always the one to go down to the registering office to make each child official. It's a father's place to do that, I feel. But then, I imagine you had to register my birth, didn't you? I'd never thought about that before. I tried to picture you as I walked in alone with my baby. I felt sure the woman in the office would think badly of me. But then, I suppose lots of women are having to register births without their menfolk around these days. If she'd heard the rumours about Stan, she never let on. In fact, she was nice as pie. It's a relief to know Susan is now a legal person. Like she actually exists. She's not just a daughter I made up for myself.

15th April 1941

Henry came home from school with a letter today. Apparently, he's been misbehaving lately—getting into fights with the boy he'd told me was his friend. The headmistress said if his behaviour doesn't improve, she'll be forced to take drastic action. Another thing to worry about.

So I sat him down in my bedroom. I didn't want to talk to him in front of Bess, or Margaret for that matter. Luckily, the daughters-in-law were off somewhere else for once. Maybe they actually do some housework occasionally. Of course, if Henry's father was here, he'd just give him a good hiding and be done with it, but I can't do that. I have to deal with the consequences, including Henry crying, David joining in, and Adam giving me the cold shoulder for being a horrible mother. To my way of thinking, if Henry's misbehaving, there's a reason. So, I asked him straight out, what's up? And to my dismay, he burst into tears. Of course, then I've got to comfort him, haven't I? I can't stay cross with my kids for long, Mama. I'm hopeless. But then I don't remember you ever getting cross with me. Maybe that's why. It turns out some kid had a go at him and told him his dad's a murderer and a yellow belly, so he decided he had to stand up for himself and show all the kids what he's made of.

I'd love to know how that story got around the town. But I think I know. I suspect I don't have to look further than a certain older woman in this house—or her sister, or maybe one of her daughters-in-law with their loose tongues. I have steam coming out my ears, but I'll bide my time in terms of how I deal with Maggie because if I don't, I don't know what I might do to her.

17ᵗʰ April 1941

I can't believe Susan is five weeks old now. She's filled out nicely, but then I would hope so, the way she guzzles the milk down. She's a pretty little thing. Not dark like you and me. More like her dad to look at. And she has that lopsided smile you can never be sure *is* a smile. It could well be wind. But she's quite contented, most of the time. I don't seem to get woken by colic as much as I did with the boys, which is just as well as I doubt Auntie Margaret would like that. I think I may have mentioned, Mama, I knitted Susan a couple of things before coming north. I had a shawl already, which I'd made for the boys. All my babies have been wrapped in that, so it's a bit of an heirloom now. I manage to keep her warm. In any case, we have some nice sunny days now, but then I don't count my chickens—it goes really chilly again at night.

20th April 1941

I got out into the garden today. It's a lovely long garden, if a bit overgrown and sloping, but it has promise, as they say. It slopes all the way down to a fence by the railway. This is the line from Keighley to Oxenhope, and I love to see the trains go by. The children and I have taken to waving at the passengers, and they all wave back. There are a couple of apple trees that might bear fruit, so long as they don't get scrumped before we can pick them. But most of the garden is grass. So much for a smallholding! There are some chicks and one female goat, which has a kid and of course eats everything going. That's going to have to be tied up if we're going to grow anything! And Lord help me, I'm going to have to get used to milking it! We need whatever nutrition we can get.

It was lovely to be out there, Mama, listening to the birds and away from the atmosphere among the women in the house. I sat on the grass and fed little Susan and then I changed her nappy out there before coming in, shielding her eyes with my body, my back to the sun. Being in the countryside, or at least not as near a big city, I notice how in the spring all the sounds seem somehow nearer. It might be because we're on a hill, facing another hill, things sprouting everywhere. I imagine it's like being in a soundproof room, not that I've ever seen one.

The other thing that lifts my spirits, Mama, even before the temperature changes or things begin to bud or birds build nests, is the smell of spring. I can't explain it, but there's a definite difference. I always say I can smell the seasons changing a good two weeks before any visible signs. Of course, those signs have been around for a few weeks now.

25th April 1941

I've had a word with Aunt Maggie and said I want to pay my way here. There's only so many times you can boil bones to make broth to have with your potatoes. I told her I've got an idea. I said I belong on the land, but obviously I don't want to just up sticks and become a land girl, because of the kids. So, I suggested I work the "smallholding" now that Susan's six weeks old. What we don't eat we can sell or barter with. I'm sure there's a thriving market for fruit, veg, and eggs. She looked doubtful. Said there's too many people have turned their back gardens into smallholdings, and besides she has to watch her hens don't get nicked as it is. But, I said, there are people who live in back to backs who can't grow veg. I told her, if we undercut the corner shop and don't ask for coupons, the women will be queuing up. Anyhow, she's agreed—I can give it a go. So, I got out there today in between feeds and washing. I'm not bothering ironing these days, I have better things to do with my time. My mum would turn in her grave, but these are not normal times. The garden's a mess! The chickens have been fed regularly, but that's about all that can be said for it. The whole area needs clearing. I started by securing the chicken fence with some wire I persuaded Auntie let me to buy from the hardware shop in town. It took a bit a time walking there and back, but it was worth it. Susan enjoyed the fresh air. I felt as if my insides were falling out after all that work. It brought the bleeding back but needs must. I'll get fitter and stronger as time goes on. There are women in some countries who don't get a lying-in period, Mama, just get straight back on with it.

Tomorrow, I'll start making rows for planting veg. And I'll begin collecting eggs. No doubt a few eggs have hatched to supply houses along this street. But that ain't happening from now on. Aggie's here. Or Frances, as I'm called in these parts. It's Uncle Harold's birthday next month, and I'm blowed if I won't bake him a cake with proper eggs in it.

28th April 1941

I've been thinking again about who might be able to help with Stan. I don't know why I didn't think of him before, but of course there's George, who brought me Stan's letter. Before he left, he gave me his address, and said, "if there's anything I can do to help any time, Mrs. Cockroft …" He never finished his sentence, and I didn't think any more about it. People often say that sort of thing without really meaning it, don't they? Let's face it, the last thing people want is a grieving widow on their hands.

I planted stuff out the back today. I've looked along the backs of houses here and I reckon people who are growing stuff might be in the running for swaps. Who knows? They might even have a few spare seeds. I've told the kids to keep the pips from their apple cores. I'm squirrelling everything I can away, Mama. I'm using old boots to grow seedlings in before I plant out. I even nicked an old rusty baking tin. Auntie Maggie didn't want me to have it, but there's no way she's going to use that old thing for baking. In the end, she gave in. Miserable old so-and-so.

I'm starting a compost heap, and everyone's potty (wee only!) from now on is to be emptied onto that. It stinks to high heaven, but it'll make good rich soil. Tea leaves go on there, and any food scraps—not that we have much left over. I'm tearing up old newspapers and any light cardboard I can lay my hands on, to help get some air into it. I've got hold of some lovely horse manure, too. I never thought I'd hear myself say those words. It's marvellous what a metal pail and an old spade can do when a horse and cart goes by and how muck can be turned into gold. Well, maybe not gold, but fed bellies. And that's all I'm interested in right now.

Today I began some tomatoes from seed, which I'll trail up against the wall. I got the kids to help me forage for nice straight sticks, and I'm collecting any twine I can—old boot laces and the like. I don't really know what I'm doing, of course. I've no idea whether I'll manage to feed us, but you've got to have a go, haven't you? We can't let Mr. Hitler win, and if we all starve that's exactly what will happen. I've also started the apple pips. I'm trying to grow an apple tree—it'll take years, though. I hope I'll be back in London by then. I persuaded Aunt Mags to let me cut up a sprouting potato and I've plonked those bits in the ground. I'll nick another one when we're next peeling!

I've cleaned the chicks out, and they look a lot happier. I've told Aunt Mags she's got to shell out for some more feed for them if she wants eggs. So, now I'm feeding them regular, and they've got a nice clean shelter. It's a start.

I also had a go at milking the goat. I got about a teaspoon. Not a very good start. I'll have to see if anyone else round here has one and get some advice. I'll throw any drips I get onto the compost until I've got the hang of it.

Our Adam came home from school today with a long face. I had to drag it out of him. He wasn't going to tell me what was up, but eventually he mumbled something about the boys having a go at him about his mum being "a darkie." So much for him having made new friends. Kids. Mind you, I'm sure these aren't the ones he's been playing out with. I've told him to point them out next time I'm with him, but he won't, of course. I'd clip their ears if I had half a chance, the little blighters. I got that when I was at school, of course. Name calling, mostly, and a bit of shoving. I got called a piccaninny. At the time, of course, it scared me to death. But I'm a mum now, and I'm bigger than these ignorant little brats. They hear this rubbish at home, I daresay.

On the plus side, Auntie Margaret now has one of her rag rugs. I need more rags, but just as soon as I get some I'll work on the others.

133

1ˢᵗ May 1941

Blimey! Here's a turn up for the books!

I was scribbling in my diary while I was waiting to see the boys' teacher, and a very nicely dressed lady came over to me. All dolled up, she was. Very posh. When she opened her mouth, she had an accent that could cut through rock better than the rapids near where we lived, Mama. Anyway, she wanted to know what I was writing. I would never go up to someone and ask something like that, but she did. It made me feel like I was back in school. For a minute, I was sure I was about to be hauled over the coals and rapped over the knuckles with a ruler. I said it was nothing, just a diary. But instead of making fun of me, she smiled, told me her name's Sheila Braithwaite, and took off her glove to shake my hand. Her nails were so clean I wanted to hide mine behind my back. I can't ever seem to get rid of the muck from working outdoors.

"So, a diary, eh? What sort of things do you write about?"

"Oh, this and that, you know," I says, shutting my book up and holding it to my chest. But my big mouth gets the better of me, of course.

"Being a widow. The kids and all their troubles. Rationing and suchlike."

"You're not from round here, are you?" She's leaning into me now, frowning. I clutch my diary even tighter.

"No. Evacuee." I'm thinking, please don't call me a darkie.

Then she smiles again, the nicest, widest smile looking straight into my eyes.

"You might just be an angel sent from heaven," she says.

Well, no one's ever called me that before! I breathed out at that point. Turns out she edits a newspaper, the Telegraph and Argus—no wonder she's posh! Half the scribblers (new word I've learned) have been called up. I daresay the editor was a man, too. She won't want to give that job up when—if—he comes back, will she?

"Would you send me some writing, about being an evacuee?" She says.

"What, me? I can't write for no newspaper," says I.

"Well, you are writing, though, aren't you?"

"That's different," I says. "No one's gonna see this, unless I die," says I, still holding it tight.

"Look, I'm not asking for an essay. It doesn't matter if the grammar isn't correct. I'll take care of that. What I want is an authentic story. Something straight from the heart. If I like it, I'll print it, but either way I'll tell you honestly what I think. What say you?"

I couldn't resist that. In for a penny, in for a pound. I'm terrified, of course, but I always was good at spelling, and my teacher used to love my stories and poems. I even wrote a play once, about a girl finding hidden treasure. The teacher said that wasn't the sort of thing girls did, and it should be a boy playing the lead, but I stuck to my guns. I didn't see why boys should have all the fun. Anyroad, I put the play on with my mates for the parents in our street, me playing the lead, and they all clapped. I reckon if this Sheila Braithwaite is going to help me be a better writer, that can only be a good thing. I've always wanted to better myself. Besides, it would make my dad proud, if he was here. I'm not counting my chickens, Mama, but she said if she prints it, she might let me write a regular slot. I got all carried away at that thought.

"From Blitz to Bradford," I says, sounding all cocky.

She's got a lovely face when she smiles; I forgot, for a moment, that I'm just an ordinary working-class girl from London, and she's a newspaper editor.

But—and here's the icing on the cake—if she prints it, she'll pay me! So, and here goes my brain working overtime as usual, if it all works out—fingers crossed, of course—I can contribute to the household income *and* grow the veg and look after the chicks. No doubt I'll still have to do some chores—Aunt Mags isn't going to let me off that lightly—but then, if I'm doing all that, she's got to let me off some of it. Time for her and me to get our heads together, I reckon.

2nd May 1941

I sat down with Aunt Maggie. For once, Bess wasn't here. She had to see the quack about her blood pressure. I made us a nice cup of tea first. I'd made some flapjacks with a bit of sugar—half what you'd normally use, mind—and butter and oats. I managed to squeeze that lot out of our rations, using bits of money I'd been given for Esther's care and a whip-round they had at Uncle Harold's local. Not that he gets there much these days, but it seems they haven't forgotten him. He handed the money over to me, since I do the shopping. Mags was in the lav at the time.

"Here, lass," he says, holding the notes out. I've not seen notes in ages.

"Tha'd best have this. I know tha'll use it wisely." He shoved it in my apron pocket before I could speak. I opened my mouth, but he made a kind of waving gesture as he turned towards his chair, calling over his shoulder:

"I shall tell t'lads tha said to thank 'em, next time I'm passing, like."

They reckon cheese rationing is coming soon, and eggs not long after, so it's just as well we have chicks. Mind you, if you keep chickens your feed will be rationed. I wouldn't mind betting milk will be on the list before the year's out. There's no sign of this madness ending any time soon.

Anyway, the flapjacks were lovely, Mama, even if I do say it myself. The generosity of good folk made them taste even sweeter. The kids loved them when they got in, too! They showed their appreciation in the usual way—by wolfing them down! So, with a nice cuppa in her hand and a flapjack to sweeten the pill, I told Aunt Mags about my

137

meeting with Sheila—Mrs. Braithwaite, that is. I told her this is proper work, but I'll need time to do it. And I told her what they'll pay; ten shillings each time they publish something. I know I'm jumping the gun, but if I do a good job, that's ten bob a week. I told her, I know she and Uncle Harold hoped I'd be having Stan's wages. I'm not sure what a war widow's pension is worth, but it doesn't look like I'll be getting one, and this is the best chance I've got of contributing some money, I said. In the land army, they get about twenty-eight shillings a week— but half of that gets taken off them immediately for food and accommodation. It might be a bit more now, but that's what it was last year—I knew a girl I went to school with who was called up for it. So, it only ends up as fourteen shillings when all's told. Let's face it, I'm Maggie and Harold's personal land army, plus I'll be bringing in money as well, fingers crossed.

Aunt Maggie was full of questions: who's going to help me (her, that is) with the washing? Who's going to help me in the kitchen (these mouths don't feed themselves you know)? What about when you have to see to Susan? Who's going to sweep the floors and dust and mop and clean the privy out?

I kept my temper. I'd already decided the best way to get her on side was for me to try and see things from her point of view. So, I said I understand. She's getting on, her house has been turned upside down. It must've been hard keeping this big house clean even before we started coming in with muddy feet, dropping crumbs. There's precious little money coming in. I think their sons Peter and Steve help out, but they have families to feed. So, money's tight. I told her I can help a lot with growing food for us and darning and mending and making do. I'm expert at making do. And I said Esther can help a bit when she gets in from school and at weekends. But I was adamant; I don't want her to be used as a skivvy. I want her to get a good education, and a childhood for goodness' sake. Aunt Mags had a face like a slapped backside, despite the sweetener. But I must have sounded pretty convincing because she saw sense (they need the money, after all!), and eventually we came to an understanding.

So, here's what's agreed. We both get up around seven. I'll be busy getting kids off to school for the first couple of hours, then I'll do my writing for an hour every day, always assuming (please, God!) this becomes regular. By ten, I'll be out back, having collected up the potties for the compost heap. I'll spend two hours out there working each day before lunch, then I'll do baking and whatever else is needed in the kitchen before the kids get in. So, I'll be gardener and chief cook, whereas Maggie will have to do most of the cleaning and shopping now. We'll share the washing up and drying, and on Mondays it's all hands to the decks for the washing. I've also told Maggie I want my boys to each have a job. She looked as if her mouth was set on catching flies when I said I'm not having them grow up thinking women's work is beneath them, even if they do earn the money when they have families of their own. I'm going to get Adam to chop, fetch, and carry wood and clean out fires. Henry can sweep their attic, and David can make sure all their clothes are put away once they're clean and aired. And they can all go off looking for wood after school. Maggie didn't bat an eyelid at the wood foraging. I suppose that's the sort of thing kids do anyway. But you could have knocked me over with a feather when Aunt Mags told me Uncle Harold, who spends all day in his chair reading the paper, has already said he'd like to help me with the smallholding. So, it's all sorted. Now, I can't wait to get writing!

4th May 1941

I told Uncle Harold my news about the Telegraph and Argus (Maggie hadn't mentioned it!), and although he never said anything, his face spread into a broad smile. His eyes seemed to shine in a way that reminded me of my mum's treasured hall table, after she'd given it a polish. She used to stand back and declare it was "shining like a sixpence on a sweep's arse." She could be surprisingly crude at times, for a God-fearing woman.

Anyway, after I told him about my job, Uncle Harold disappeared upstairs and came down blowing dust off two big old books.

"I've no use for these mesen, lass. They're yours," he said, sounding gruff as he passed them over.

And so, Mama, I now have a dictionary, and something called a thesaurus. I'll think of them as a loan. I don't like taking things from people, but I do like the thesaurus. There are so many ways to say something! What I like most about writing is, when you play with words, they seem to sing to you. Like you used to sing to me, Mama. When I read or write a story, I snuggle up in a warm, colourful and scented story-garden, with word-music sung by angels.

I'm reading a lot to try and better myself, though I talk rough and probably always will. That's a hard habit to crack. When I'm writing, I can take my time to select the right word or phrase—whereas when I'm talking, words seem to fall over each other in an effort to get out. Uncle Harold has lots of books, and I'm working my way through them. Plus, there's the library here in Keighley. I'm finding new authors I hadn't even heard of before, like John Steinbeck (he's American and writes about ordinary working men) and Aldous Huxley who wrote something called *Brave New World*, all about how awful life could be in the future, if we're not careful. They're opening new dream-worlds for me. I don't seem to need to travel so often to see you now, though I'll never forget you, and I'll always love you and miss you, Mama. It's just that in those moments after my work is done and I am finally alone, books are the worlds into which I journey.

I'm working hard in the garden. I've found out what I need to do to get milk out of the goat. The kid has died, so I must keep the milk supply going. Luckily, there's a fella called Fred down the road who has one, and he's given me some tips. Best thing, apparently, is to put a treat in front of her while I milk her—something like oats and evaporated milk. Of course, both my hands and the goat's underbelly need to be squeaky clean. I've borrowed Uncle Harold's razor to shave her. I've also got hold of an old bench, to which I can strap her with a belt of Uncle Harold's that's seen better days. There's no way she'll stay still, otherwise—even with the treat. Anyway, Mama, wish me luck! I'm having a go tomorrow!

5th May 1941

Success! I have half a pint of goat's milk, which is better than none! I must remember to keep my hands high up and not squeeze the end of the teat (otherwise I get kicked!), plus I need to relax and get into a rhythm, but I think I might get the hang of it.

I gave the boys and Auntie Margaret a little taster. They all pulled a face, but I put some in my tea. It's fine so long as you don't use too much. I'll put it in cakes and porridge. I bet I can get it past them.

8th May 1941

Mama, I've made two new friends. They were sat on the bank on the other side of the railway when I was out in the garden, and they waved at me, big smiles and all. They're obviously land girls judging by what they were wearing. They must've been on their break because they each had a sandwich wrapped in brown paper. Anyway, I could hardly ignore them, so I waved back. They're Millie, who's slight, and Cath, who's taller. God knows how Millie does heavy work. No sooner had they said their names than they called to say they had to go. As they ran off up the bank Cath called over her shoulder:

"See you tomorrow!" as if it were a given.

The next day, I did see them again. Cath asked me what my name is, so I said Frances, and she said they'd call me Frankie. So now I have another name. From the name you gave me Mama, to Frances to Agnes and back to Frances, now Frankie! Never a dull moment.

Cath keeps her hair short. Sensible for the kind of work they're doing. Millie's hair falls in lovely soft curls that don't seem to want to be constrained by her scarf. I watched as they went back to work holding hands, the way girls do—swinging them back and forth. Such an odd couple, with Cath being so much taller than Millie, but they're obviously great pals. They kissed each other on the lips before they set off, like mother and daughter.

11ᵗʰ May 1941

Today, I went down to the railway line, so that as soon as I might spot Cath and Millie, we'd be able to chat a bit. It's nice to meet some women my own age. I saw them coming over the hill, and they clocked me too, waved as if I was an old friend and sat down in what I imagine must be their usual spot. I crossed the tracks to join them this time.

It turns out, Millie had a husband who was very recently killed in action. When I offered my condolences, I got a bit of a shock. She smiled at Cath as she squeezed her hand:

"I'm glad to be rid of him."

"Why?" I asked, my mouth getting ahead of my brainbox as usual.

She turned and looked at me like she was searching for something in my soul—an anchor to hold onto.

"He was a drunk. Hit me."

"Oh," says I. "My Stan would never do that. He says men like that are spineless."

Me and my big mouth. They both just looked at me. I might as well have just said that two and two make fifty-five.

Anyway, no harm seems to have been done, thankfully. The girls have invited me to a dance! Apparently, the land girls have a dance every Saturday night. No men allowed. Should be fun. So, I'm going, Saturday week. I need to ask Esther if she'll mind looking out for the kids. Luckily, Susan has started sleeping through after her evening feed, the little angel. She never makes a fuss—not like her brothers were, at all!

143

12th May 1941

There's a woman along the road called Edie. She's lost all her menfolk in this bloody war. Husband and three sons. And yet there are crooks in London who've dodged call-up and happily put on ARP arm bands to load up the contents of a shop which they'll sell later on the black market. Evil sods like that seem to live, whereas poor Edie's man and sons don't. Aunt Mags told me, but instead of her usual salacious (new word there, Mama. I'm using my thesaurus!) tone when she's putting her two penn'orth in about someone, her eyes were wet. She looked anywhere but at me, and her voice sounded as if she'd borrowed someone else's, and it didn't quite fit.

15th May 1941

I started writing my article for the Telegraph and Argus, and I couldn't stop until I'd finished a first draft! It needs tidying, but I'm quite pleased with it, even though I says it as shouldn't. Let's hope Sheila Braithwaite likes it. Of course, I had to use my best handwriting and check my spelling in the dictionary once or twice. I slipped in one or two new-to-me words. What got me thinking is this war.

It's strange. I'm used to a man telling me what to do and being the boss, but I'm not sure I could go back to that now. I hope my Stan is alive, but if he is, and my hope wears thinner every day like a shoelace that's been tied too many times, then I shall have to make some changes. I'm not the same woman I was when he went away, not by a long chalk. For a start, I've lost one child and had another. I thought the pain of losing our little Stephen would bring on early labour, so I'd lose two instead of one, but I'm tougher than I realised. Look at what I coped with during the Blitz. Nightly raids, making sure the kids were alright. Taking on Esther. I didn't even bother arguing with myself on that one! And then the decision to travel north with all the children, with me in a delicate condition. I'm getting used to making decisions now. I never thought I would. But I quite like it. And now there's the garden. I planned it out, went along the road to beg neighbours for things to start us off, and I did the hard graft. Uncle Harold saw that I meant business and asked if he could help. Asked mind. To help, not to take over.

So, *From Blitz to Bradford*, first episode is all about how I, an ordinary woman, have been changed by this war. How I've had to start making decisions, how I'm stronger than I thought, and how I'm learning new skills.

Which reminds me, Mama. Cath and Millie have said if they get any shoots they would be throwing out, they'll give some to me. I've already started thinning mine. Nothing is wasted. I put the ones I can't use either on the compost heap or save them for old Bert down the road so I can do swaps.

18th May 1941

The dance was terrific! We did all the old favourites—waltz, foxtrot, charleston. Even the quickstep, though I was useless. It turns out Cath's a really good dancer and doesn't mind taking the lead, so she taught me tons. I came home with a face ache from smiling so much, Mama! I got back around ten and collapsed into bed. Had the best sleep ever, until Susan wanted feeding at five. I've told Esther if Auntie Maggie doesn't mind listening out for the kids she can come to the next one, her being thirteen now. She's nearly old enough to go to work, so she can get the feel of what it would be like to be a land girl.

Oh, and guess what, Mama! Mrs. Braithwaite liked my article! Of course, she's changed the odd word here and there and found better ways to say what I was trying to, but it's my story. She came round yesterday, which was hilarious. Bess and Maggie were falling over themselves to make her comfortable, offering cups of tea and the pouffe for her feet. She wants me to do a weekly article, and she'll sort me out a typewriter! I'll feel like a proper writer, with one of those! Mind you, it'll take a while to get used to it.

19th May 1941

I wrote quite a while ago to George, and also again to that Lieutenant, who must be getting royally sick of me. Having heard nothing from either, I got George's reply in the first post and the Lieutenant's in the second today—like London buses, Mama. You wait forever, then two come at once. Here's what George said:

Dear Mrs. Cockroft,

I am absolutely certain your Stan was innocent, and I am also equally certain I know who did it.

If there is any way I can help at all, including writing letters of support or indeed appearing as a character witness in any posthumous re-trial, do let me know. They didn't call me as a witness. I think they felt there was sufficient evidence against him, and they weren't looking for any other explanations.

There is something I didn't mention when I came to see you to deliver Stan's letter. I was so concerned that I should deliver it safely, I wanted to spare you the details. But it's time to put things right. I overheard the cook—the one I am sure did It—talking to another chap the night before that poor boy died. He said quite clearly:

*"I've had enough of that little runt. He has too much heart and not enough b***s. I'm gonna do for him and kill two birds with one meat cleaver."*

I never told anyone, but maybe I should have. I hope you'll forgive me.

Yours sincerely,

George (Nolan)

I didn't like that word, posthumous. But I wrote straight back to him and begged him to contact the authorities with what he knows.

When the one from the Lieutenant came it was briefer, but just what I needed to hear:

> *Dear Mrs. Cockroft,*
>
> *I fully appreciate that you would like the chance to clear your husband's name. You must understand, however, that he was tried and found guilty. The only circumstances under which a posthumous retrial could occur would be if significant new evidence had come to light.*
> *Sincerely,*
> *Lieutenant Commander Arthur Wright*

So, the Lieutenant has had a promotion. Having rushed off a letter to George, I sent another to the Lieutenant Commander to tell him I have a witness who wasn't called to the trial and has vital evidence. I copied out word for word what George said, mentioned it was a sailor who had been retired due to injury, and told him I'd supply George's name and address once I had his permission. Now I wait! I'm like a kid, anxiously hoping for her dream Christmas present, even if summer is around the corner.

20th May 1941

Well, the post is certainly doing overtime, Mama. It's hard to get to the doormat when it arrives, mind you. Aunt Mags usually pushes past me, and when she's picked it up, Bess wants a look, as if she lived here. Today, some nice news, and some expected but not so nice. I've heard for certain I won't get a widow's pension, but I also heard from Hilda, with lots of news about what's happening in London. The bombs are still falling, some people still occasionally demonstrate for the Peace Pledge Union, but from the reception they get you'd think they were spitting on the graves of the people who are dying in this ruddy war, instead of trying to campaign to stop it and find other ways than mass slaughter to do battle with Hitler and his mob. To be fair, I didn't realise there are other ways to do things than rush off to war, before I met Hilda—ways that don't involve killing innocent people on both sides. I never stopped to think there might be decent people in Germany. I saw them all as the evil enemy, because that's what we're told. Even German Jews who escaped from Hitler were shoved in jail, and I was there with the rest of the good British people, calling them all the names under the sun. But they aren't all evil, are they? The men and women in the street have been sold a lie, just like a substandard bit of meat off the market. They've been told, just like we have, that certain other people are bad and want to take over the world. In their case it's the Jews they think are behind all the world's troubles, but I bet they hate us British just as much as we hate them. They probably think they're the goodies! It never occurred to me before I got talking to Hilda, and Ruth, and the others, just how but for the grace of God it could be me sitting there in my house in Berlin or Bavaria, hitting the table and swearing about the English—

and believing it. Now I know what I know, I can't hate all Germans. I hate Hitler, though. There do seem to be some evil people in the world, but the best way to stop them is to spot what they're up to and nip it in the bud. Not that I would know how to do that, mind—but diplomats and such-like, they should be doing that sort of thing.

But we British didn't shut the stable door when we should have, so Hitler's in power, waging war and invading countries. We need to stop him invading ours. He's in Greece now. We can't get out of this war now it's in full swing. He must not set foot on this soil. In the meantime, people need to be educated about these things—to have their eyes opened, just like I have—and then people won't vote for monsters like Hitler in the first place. Then his ilk won't get the power they crave, to do evil acts like murdering Jews so that poor Esther and other children like her had to escape over here, in the certain knowledge that their parents suffered a worse fate. When I look at her, I fancy I can see a gaping hole inside where her mother once was. I should know. I'm her Ma, but not the mother I'm sure she pines for.

Hilda's husband, Paul, is risking life and limb with the Friends Ambulance Service. She's so proud of him, Mama. He's a truly brave man with no weapon at his side to defend himself, going behind enemy lines to pick up the injured and bring them to safety. I know she worries about him, but she puts a brave face on it. Poor Nathan, Ruth's husband, is of course a POW, so it is difficult to know what'll come of him, especially with him being a Jew. But at least small comfort for her is that he isn't having to go up in the air on a daily basis and not come down one day. Rebecca and Chaim miss him terribly, Hilda says, but Ruth keeps them going with stories of their daddy's bravery. She still observes the Sabbath every Friday night. Then there's Sandhya's husband. He's no longer a lawyer. He's probably driving tanks somewhere in North Africa. He's in the army, anyway.

I'm beginning to enjoy my life in the outdoors here now spring is well and truly underway, but I do miss my friends in London. I don't miss those ruddy bombs though! Even Buckingham Palace was hit on March 8. No one's safe, not even royalty! Plymouth's getting it, too; I suppose because of the navy being down there, and Bristol's taken a bashing—not to mention Glasgow, where they make our ships.

21ˢᵗ *May 1941*

That Winston Churchill certainly knows how to give a good speech. I daresay you've heard him, Mama. We were all crowded round the wireless today, listening to him just like we were last August, just before the Blitz started, when he praised our pilots who fought in the Battle of Britain:

"Never in the field of human conflict was so much owed by so many to so few."

He definitely has a way with words, that man. Of course, he'd rallied them all just a few months before. He told us our British way of life depended on our men's efforts, and if we failed, we would all fall into a dark abyss, but if we won people would say, "This was their finest hour." Hilda later said he's a good orator. I never knew what the word meant, but she educated me about how easily we can be swayed by a good speech. Of course, that's also what Hitler's doing, with the German people.

22nd May 1941

I managed to collect enough eggs to make a nice big cake for Uncle Harold's birthday, Mama. Of course, with sugar and jam rationed I had to be clever. Butter being rationed, I had to make do with very little fat, but I had some stewed apples that made the cake lovely and moist. Everyone agreed it was lovely, and even if there was only enough tea for a weak cup each, we did alright. At least milk isn't rationed. Yet. After we'd all sung happy birthday, Uncle Harold glanced at me with such a lovely warm look in his eyes; I thought for a minute he might cry. Then, when we were washing up, Maggie actually thanked me for making his day. Well, I never.

I think I'll write about cooking on rations, for Mrs. Braithwaite. She'll like that, I reckon.

I've met some people right here in Keighley from the Peace Pledge Union! I noticed them in the town square, with placards supporting conscientious objectors. I can't understand why the Union went out of favour, when they were so popular in 1934. They merged in 1937 with No More War, which apparently began in 1921. All the pacifists I've met seem to be motivated by a deep conviction, often Christian—though in Ruth's case, you might say it's her humanity. I met someone today who told me about a chap called Eric Stephenson, with links both to this area and to Woolwich. He registered as a conscientious objector in Bradford. He was working in Halfords in Godwin Street when war was declared, and he didn't like the way his boss raised the price of torch bulbs to make a quick bob. Apparently, Eric sold them at the old price until he got found out. Anyway, he'd sat the civil service exam while still at school and so last year he was sent to the Ministry of Supply—at Woolwich Arsenal. He did his first aid and was volunteering at St Nicholas hospital on the male wards in addition to his official work, but then he decided to train as a nurse. He was living on Plumstead common and worshipping with Quakers, so I expect Hilda knows him. Small world, Mama. Just not small enough for me to bump into you when I go shopping.

There are now approaching sixty thousand conscientious objectors. Not all of them manage to convince the tribunals, though, so about three thousand are in prison. Still, at least they're safe there, or relatively so. That is, so long as they're not beaten up by crooks while the screws turn a blind eye. Some pacifists have gone into social work—the welfare, as most people call it. Others go into farming or forestry. Many, like Eric

Stephenson, look after the sick and wounded. Some have volunteered for clearing unexploded bombs. Like I say, they're anything but lazy or cowards—but that is what they get called. That, and traitors. Apparently, even when they are allowed to keep their existing jobs they might get the sack. My editor, Mrs. Braithwaite, said the BBC has dismissed all its conscientious objectors. She got wind of my links with the PPU and has asked me to do an article on pacifism, so the cookery article will have to wait. Mind you, I'm not sure I want to show my colours; people could be baying for my blood. But it's another ten bob. I can't really turn it down. I'll interview people this time, starting with the local Quakers.

I'm slowly getting used to this typewriter, Mama, though I know I could write much faster by hand. Oh, well, onwards and upwards!

24th *May 1941*

It's really beginning to warm up now, Mama. Which of course means rain! Harold and I work our socks off in the garden, him hobbling around with his stick, but it's paying off. We're beginning to get some lovely vegetables, which all helps. That, and the eggs and goat's milk. I know the milk tastes funny and isn't everyone's cup of tea, but I don't mind it, and I've even had a go at making some soft cheese with it. It's very good. But then, I like strong tastes.

After everyone had gone to bed last night, I stayed downstairs. I like it when it's quiet and I can just soak up the peace. Each night I thank my lucky stars to be away from those bombs, and I say a silent prayer for all those who are living through a bombing that night, as well as for my Stan and all the blokes who are facing the nightly terrors of war. Anyway, I must have drifted off, or maybe I didn't. But pretty soon, I was somewhere I've never been before.

I'm somewhere near Euston Station, at the centre of a big building. I'm part of a group of maybe fifty people, all sitting in a circle, in complete silence. Some people are frowning, like they're trying really hard to think about something. Others have the kind of look you associate with one of the pictures of the saints - a kind of other-worldly look, not a line on their faces no matter how old, as if someone had come along with an iron and smoothed all the wrinkles out, along with their worries. I'm overcome with a sense of calm. It's almost as if you could reach out and touch the peace, or as if it is touching me— wrapping me into itself, like a big warm and loving cloak.

I must have stayed there a while, but then I realised it was time to get to bed so I forced my legs up the apples and pears, hoping not to wake anyone as the old wooden stairs groaned almost as much as Maggie does when she has to bend down. I slept like a log.

25th May 1941

Today, I started working on my new article. Not the cookery one, Mama, but the one about peace groups. I went and called into the Quaker Meeting in Keighley just as they were ending their worship and had a word with the first person I saw when I walked through the door. I never would have done that, nine months ago. Stan always did all the talking for me when he was here. As a kid, I used to literally hide behind my mum's skirts when someone strange came in the room or when she stopped to talk to anyone at a bus stop or in Woolwich market. Now look at me, Mama! I'm turning up in new places and starting a conversation!

I managed to get a few names of people who are active in the peace movement here, and I've arranged to go back Wednesday to see them all. They seemed delighted that someone wants to do an article about what they believe in. Let's hope it doesn't result in bricks being thrown through our windows. Maggie's only just started warming to me.

27th May 1941

I still see the two land girls, Cath and Millie, most days and stop and chat, and I've been to a few more dances since I first met them. I even managed to get Esther along with me to one, though she was painfully shy, bless her, and said afterwards she'd rather look after my lot. It's so nice to be able to mix with people my own age, Mama. Cath and Millie always dance with each other, while the rest of us mingle around the hall, continually changing partners. I don't care whether I lead or follow, to be honest—so long as I get to dance!

I think I've worked out what Cath and Millie are, Mama, not wishing to offend your sensibilities. I've heard about their sort of course, but never actually met anyone that way out before. Or at least, if I have, I didn't realize. Who can blame them for finding love in this crazy war? I'm not about to go around criticizing them. I think they've decided they can trust me, and I'm glad. At our last dance on Saturday, they were talking about when this war is over maybe buying a place together with a small holding and just carrying on doing what they're doing. Good on them, I said. I wish I had someone to love, I said, and they smiled at me as Cath pulled her arm a bit tighter round Millie.

I wonder if Stan will ever come back? I'm beginning to think he won't, and this is it. I'm a widow without a widow's pension, having to work to make ends meet and feed my kids. Little Susan's definitely smiling now and making movements with her mouth as if she's trying to talk. I'm besotted with her—she comes outside with me when I'm working. She's quite protected from rain and wind in the pram, so she gets lots of fresh air. In fact, it's just got quite warm, so things are looking up. The lettuces are lovely.

28ᵗʰ *May 1941*

Today I interviewed three Quakers. Such lovely people. One of them reminded me of Hilda, very nicely spoken and probably in her forties. It was hard to understand her. She was very quietly spoken. I wish I could do shorthand like a real scribbler. Maybe I'll learn it when the war's over. She said she's something called a birthright Quaker. She went to a Quaker boarding school. Barbaric practice, separating children from their parents if you ask me, but she seemed not to feel she'd missed out. Sadly, she wasn't all that helpful on the peace message, other than to direct me to their peace testimony. That says they're against all outward wars, because Jesus taught us to love our enemies. One of the other Quakers helped me out—an elderly gentleman called Ernest. He said loving one's enemies is an "abstract concept" (difficult to understand idea, I think he meant—it's not like having a cake recipe, is it?) that some people find it very hard to do, but one way to think about it in times of war is that there are children of God on both sides, doing and believing what they're told. That bit made sense. I'd already worked it out for myself, as you know, mostly thanks to Hilda. The other lady was also older, married to the gentleman, I think. She just nodded her head whenever he spoke, right up until the end, when she quietly led me to their little library and produced a pamphlet with words I can copy out for my article—words that George Fox (who founded the Religious Society of Friends, what we know as Quakers) and others used nearly three hundred years ago:

"That spirit of Christ by which we are guided is not changeable, so as once to command us from a thing as evil and again to move unto it; and we do certainly know, and so testify to the world, that the spirit of

Christ, which leads us into all Truth, will never move us to fight and war against any man with outward weapons, neither for the kingdom of Christ, nor for the kingdoms of this world."

Powerful words. I wish I had that sort of conviction. It made me think how different their attitude is from our vicar in London, who was preaching peace right up to war being declared, then suddenly he was all for war.

She told me to "keep it at your leisure," though I'll make sure I give it back as soon as I can. She also invited me to join them on Sunday for worship. And do you know what? I might just do that.

3ʳᵈ June 1941

I've been really busy, what with writing and looking after veggies and goat and kids (haha! Kids, get it? Baby goats).

I wrote my article about Quakers and peace, and there it was right across the page, printed with my name on it! They call that a by-line. It was much longer than my previous piece, and harder to write, but it was really interesting to do. I told Sheila I can do more about peace issues if she wants. I have no idea how it'll go down, of course. It's not exactly a popular topic, when the daily papers are running stories with headlines like, "The Germans are on the run!" and "We showed them!" I can't think Keighley's going to have a rush on membership for the PPU, nor the Religious Society of Friends, and I still don't know exactly how I feel about it all myself. Still, I tried to do honest, unbiased reporting.

Aunt Margaret knows someone who was a secretary before she got married, and she's going to train me to touch type. I feel nervous, because she will have to teach me here in the living room. No doubt Bess will comment all the way through!

4th June 1941

I'm learning a lot from Sheila about how to structure my writing. You tell the story in the first paragraph, because busy people might not read the rest of it. You also have to hook them in, so it has to be catchy. They love puns, do reporters. They seem to like their beer quite a lot, too. One young scribbler who's back at the paper after having his foot blown off suggested I call in for a cheeky half with him. It was only one o'clock, and in any case, I'd left Susan with Mags, quite apart from me being a married woman, so I said no thanks.

Am I still a married woman? I don't know, to be honest Mama. I'm told Stan's dead, but I still refuse to believe it. At least, I refuse to think about it until I've cleared his name.

9th June 1941

Esther is turning into a fine young woman. Her eyes are like warm, dark almonds and her skin such a beautiful sandy colour, without the blemishes I remember having at that age. Despite being thin, her lips are full and have that natural red young girls have. I'm concerned she might attract the wrong kind of attention from boys. I'm doing the worrying her mother would have done if only she were here. I feel her with me, like wind at my back urging me to do her work as best I can. I see it as service—a kind of homage to those lost souls harangued or worse just for belonging to a group that has so often been treated as different and dangerous. I'm reminded of poor Ruth's parents, escaping the pogroms not so many years ago. And now this. It seems people have been taking pot shots at Jews for all eternity.

Esther's teacher asked to have a word with me this week. By rights, Esther should be preparing to leave school once she turns fourteen in December, bringing in a wage to help support this household. But the teacher tells me she thinks Esther could be a doctor one day. It's hard for girls to get into any university, let alone for medicine. But she reckons if Esther does want to be a doctor, the best place for her is London School of Medicine for Women. She's convinced Esther is up to it. I didn't know, but there are scholarships available for girls from poorer backgrounds, through something called Soroptimists International. It's a network of clubs around the world that try to give women and girls a better future. The one in Britain was set up in the twenties, for girls who had no mother. Apparently, they are also motivated by the peace message and have a special interest in refugees. Her teacher, unbeknownst to me, is a member of these Soroptimists and sees Esther as a deserving cause. A lady doctor in the family, eh? Whatever next? Not that I can take any credit, mind, given that she is not my blood. But, and this was the bombshell, her teacher says she might need to go away to school where they can give her more help than they can here. She could see whether there's a local grammar school that might take her, but Esther could sit a scholarship examination to get into a private school, all fees and board and so on paid for. They give children a better chance of getting into university, but are further away, so she'd have to board. When I heard that, Mama, my throat went tight, and I had to look away to compose myself. Like I say, I know I didn't give birth to this girl. I only met her a few months ago, but I've protected her like one of my own, and if I'm honest, I've grown to love her as if she were my daughter. Silly me. I forgot she's not actually mine and one day she might leave me.

One thing this has taught me though, is that I now understand how easily you can grow to love a child that isn't your blood. I think I just learned how much my mum probably loved me.

10th June 1941

Well, I decided, in fairness to Esther, I should tell her what the teacher told me. Surprise, surprise—she wants to learn all she can, and she's keen to have a bash at becoming a doctor. It turns out her dad was a doctor, and her mum a nurse. I'd no idea. How could those Nazis kill anyone, let alone a doctor and nurse, just for being Jewish?

I think the teacher must have spoken to her already, because she didn't seem surprised. In fact, she told me it's her dream to become a children's doctor before I mentioned it.

So, her teacher, Mrs. Day, has arranged an interview, and there's a small test she has to take the same day. Mrs. Day offered to take her herself, but I said no. That's my job as her guardian. I've asked if Aunt Mags can look after the kids after school, and she's agreed. Of course, Susan will have to come with us. It'll be a long day, but I'll feel so proud of Esther if she gets in. What a wonderful opportunity! Even if I do doubt the wisdom of sending children away to school. Maybe, in Esther's case, it's the best thing. I hope she doesn't forget me. I've grown so fond of her. But how could I deny her this chance of a better life than I ever dreamed of for myself, or for any of mine come to that matter? She's a lovely girl, and she's been through so much. There was a lightness in her movements when we discussed it, as if someone just lit a fire inside her. I'm not about to put it out, that's for sure.

165

12th June 1941

Our David was seven today. I can hardly believe he's grown so big, and it's good to have a happy event. I baked some biscuits, and he was as pleased as punch.

Of course, I had to stop Bess and the other two eating more than one each before he got home. Luckily, there were enough to go round, with an extra one for the birthday boy.

16th June 1941

Esther's had her interview. It was a pig of a journey. I had to take a couple of bags with nappies and sandwiches and water, so I was loaded down. But Esther helped me carry. She's such a good girl. Oh, my gosh! I am going to miss her if she gets in, but I'm not about to stand in her way. There's many that would, of course, thinking she owed them, but I reckon if she can do well, I will take pleasure as much as if I'd done it myself.

The school's very grand—a big old house with oak this and oak that. Wide staircase, and heavy doors. She had to sit all alone to take her test in a cavernous, draughty room with enormous sash windows. I was allowed to see her straight after. Me and Susan—Susan and I—went for a little walk round the grounds, which were lovely. It was a nice sunny day, thankfully. We've had a bit of rain of late, but there wasn't a cloud in the sky. The grounds are very extensive. They've got their own tennis courts and there's a lot of plants and a little pond with frogs and fish in it, with a dainty little bridge over. There's even a building I'm told is a swimming pool! After the exam (it turned out the test wasn't so little, after all) was out the way they wanted to see us together, then we were given a tour of the grounds, plus we saw a classroom and dormitory. There's a sick bay, too of course, a big hall for assemblies and dinners, and a gymnasium with horse, mats, and ropes. The usual sort of thing, but all out of the league of my kids' little local school. The floors and window ledges were spotless.

It took three trains to get there, but we were picked up at the other end by a school bus, thankfully, then dropped back at the station afterwards to start our journey home. On the way from Leeds to

Keighley we all fell asleep and nearly missed our stop! Maggie saved us some tea, but we were both so exhausted I struggled eating it, and I could tell Esther did, too. I asked if I could save my dessert for today's lunch, and Esther quickly said what a good idea that was and could she have hers when she got in from school.

I had to crack on with typing after everyone was in bed, despite wanting to give up and get between the sheets myself. One thing I can say, though, is it's now getting easier, since I've been typing every day, and I no longer need the lessons. Hoorah!

17th June 1941

Today, my poor little Stephen would have been six. I've not reminded the children of the date, and none of them remembered. I've just said a little prayer down in the garden for his soul and gone about the day as best I could, but I know Aunt Margaret noticed something was amiss because she kept looking at me funny.

21st June 1941

Summer's definitely here. The garden's doing nicely. Just as well, as rationing's even tighter. Cheese last month, but at least I can make a soft goat's cheese. This month, eggs. We've got a few hens now though—plenty of eggs. Mind you, the feed is rationed, as expected. We often give food away to families in need, but we have to keep some of our surplus back for bartering. It's the only way to do things in this stupid war.

I'm reading reports of what seems to be an end to the Blitz. There haven't been nightly bombings since last month. I suppose I could go home now, but it seems a shame to leave what I've built up here. I mean, I'm contributing to the household income, I'm a bona fide journalist with several articles to my name and a regular column, I've got a bit of land to grow vegetables and keep chickens and the goat on, whereas I'd have to start all over again in Plumstead, and much as I miss my friends there, I've become quite fond of Cath, Millie, Uncle Harold—and even Aunt Mags, though I never thought I'd hear myself say it. Plus, I think they've grown fond of me. Mags was a hard nut to crack, but she's softened up a lot. The kids are thriving here, too. There's loads of land to play on and they love making dens. After school they just take off. Mind you, I suppose they could do that in the woods behind our house in Plumstead. I don't know if I want to go. I don't know if I have a choice.

And then there's Esther. She's got into that school, and she'll be starting in September. It's a long way for her to come back to us in the holidays if we're in London, and I worry once she's no longer sharing a bed with me whether the nightmares and tummy pains will start again.

At least it's a girl's school. I wish Stan was here to advise me.

All this talk of Plumstead and of Esther reminds me of my own days as a carefree girl. Mind you, I stopped being carefree the day I turned fourteen and had to go out to work. Before that, my brother David and me (I, sorry) used to go off to Danson Park or Charlton Lido in the summer and stay all day with a loaf of bread between us and a bottle of water. We always got thirsty, so we refilled it at the taps, even though it wasn't drinking water. But we didn't care. We'd jump and push each other into the water, and lark about in the pool for hours. Poor David would go red and peel but I never did, thanks to my complexion. How I miss the days when I thought there'd never be anything more to worry about than whether my tummy was full.

23rd *June 1941*

Well, that ruddy Hitler's gone and invaded Russia, who were their allies! All's fair in love and war, or so they say, though I don't agree. I've never met a Russian, or come to that a German, apart from Esther who I don't count, what with her being Jewish. Come to that, Ruth's parents were Russian, but they were hounded out.

None of us asked for this war, did we really? Especially the women. It's men making the decision to go to war, isn't it? The other day, I was stood in a queue in the market for some fish, next to a lady I recognised from the school. We got chatting about this and that—kids, the weather, rationing. I expected her to mention me digging for victory when I told her I'd taken over the smallholding, but instead she just looked ahead of her and said:

"You do realise, love, it's not us women have made this war."

Soon after coming here, I remember the white feathers some women dished out to young men, all pious like. They made you feel guilty if you hadn't volunteered. There were plenty of young men shamed into joining up—some who lied about their age so they wouldn't be called yellow bellies. So, women might not be making this war, but there's a darned sight too many that are gung-ho about it.

Still, it made me think. It's powerful men sitting down there in Number 10 Downing Street and the Houses of Parliament making the laws and deciding whether we go to war or not. And it's powerful men—toffs—in charge of the forces, giving the orders to fight or drop bombs or whatever. While the rest of us pay the price. Young men are cannon fodder, while women, children and old people lose sons, husbands, lovers and daddies. And get bombed for their trouble.

24th June 1941

Well, I can't believe it. A letter came this morning from the Rear Admiral, no less! Now that is one powerful man:

Dear Mrs. Cockroft,

I would like to inform you that we have received new evidence to suggest your husband may have been innocent of the crime of which he was convicted some months ago.

I can therefore advise you that the verdict has been changed postmortem to Not Guilty.

I will inform the war office of this decision.

Please accept my congratulations.

Yours sincerely,

[Unreadable signature],

Rear Admiral

So, Stan's name has been cleared, probably thanks to that nice gentleman, George Nolan, coming forward. I'm guessing it was him that provided the new evidence. I hardly had to do a thing in the end. How our fortunes can change in an instant. But it has made me cry for my poor, dear Stan, who never got to hear of this verdict.

When I have got over the shock, I think I'll ask Sheila to run a story on it.

25ᵗʰ June 1941

I keep reading that letter from the Rear Admiral. I've gone from feeling as pleased as punch, to crying, to twisting my apron around my fingers, unable to rest easy.

How dare he congratulate me, yet not apologise? I've faced humiliation. Stan died knowing his innocence, but never believed by others.

Last night, in my dreams, I went on another one of my travels to somewhere I didn't recognise.

The grass is the most vibrant green I've ever seen, and the blue-green of the rivers reminds me of my childhood on the other side of the world—like it could be cut into gemstones to wear round your neck. All the colours are so alive, it's as if someone's separated them out and given them each a good clean, then held them to the light.

I'm unsurprised to find Stan with me. It's as if we were never separated. He sits on the grass and pats beside him.

"I have something to say to you, my darling Aggie, and I need you to listen very carefully."

I feel his touch on my hand, like a feather in the wind, and then both his hands on my face, curling my hair round my ears. I notice a look in his eyes of sorrow, and at the same time love. His voice is soft and low, making me long to be alone with him in our bed.

I make an effort to tidy those thoughts away and listen, to be a good, obedient wife. I see little droplets forming in his eyes, tears I've never in all our years of marriage seen him shed. A feeling of dread grips the pit of my stomach. I want to put my fingers in my ears so I don't have to hear what's coming next, but my hands won't move.

"It's time to let go, Agnes."

"No! No! I will never let go of you!"

I think, if I bargain, if I play for time, maybe I can hold onto this moment where the colours are bright with hope, and we're together. Maybe we can start all over again, make a new home in this place of dreams and beauty.

"Agnes, I cannot return."

He leans forward, holding my hair to my ears and kissing my forehead.

"I'm somewhere else now. I will always love you, and I'm so sorry I had to leave, but it was my time. Please give my love to the children, and tell them their daddy will always love them and care for them—including Susan."

I shut my eyes as he holds my head. I want to feel his hands enveloping me, forever. If I hold this moment, nothing can harm me.

Then I opened my eyes, and Esther was snoring next to me. As I looked at her delicate little face, I realised she hasn't had a nightmare for a while. At least that's one good thing. The light was peering round the curtains, making fun of me for sleeping late. I got up and washed my face, my heart lying in my chest like one of the heavy rocks in those dark, Yorkshire dry stone walls.

26th June 1941

I've felt a deep pain since Stan said I must let him go, Mama, akin to the desperation I felt at sea, after they took me from you. I know I've felt my husband's touch for the last time. He's dead. I'm a widow.

But I must keep going, for the children. I've managed to finish all the rag rugs, so now everyone has one again, and Aunt Mags has her two.

I can't afford to wallow. We've had bad news about Uncle Harold, Mama. He has a heart condition. Sadly, this means he mustn't work with me in the garden anymore. He's been getting breathless, and eventually we scraped together the money for him to see the quack. I walked with him, so he had someone to hold onto. He didn't want to make a fuss, but I insisted, and Maggie looked pleased that I had. She's not as young and strong as me. There's no way she could have held him if he'd collapsed, whereas I've got biceps a man would be proud of.

I sat in while the doc listened to Uncle Harold's chest and gave him the once over. I didn't take to the doctor. He didn't look Uncle Harold in the eye when he spoke. Plus, he had an unpleasant wart on one cheek. I know you can't judge a book by its cover, but it added to his overall look, which was what you might call overpowering. His eyebrows met in the middle, too, and needed a trim if you ask me. I didn't much appreciate his attempt at humour, either.

"It's time you stopped chasing the girls, Harry," he said, sounding way too familiar for my liking. At least give him his proper title, I thought. This man fought in the last war and lost a leg for the likes of you. But I kept my trap shut.

"Your heart's giving out old boy," was his next attempt at a bedside manner. "Time to put your feet up in the few months you've got left."

So, that's how you tell a man he's dying, is it? I could feel myself getting hot under the collar, fidgeting on one of those hard seats.

"Hang on a minute," says I, opening my big mouth. "Can't you do some tests? How can you be sure, just from listening to him?"

He looked at me as if a wasp had entered his consulting room, and he needed to swat me away with snide words.

"Madam," says he, looking at my ring finger to check. "I've been doing this job for more years than you've had hot dinners," says he. "I know heart failure when I hear it."

"It's alright, Frances," says Uncle Harold, patting my hand and sounding like he's trying to reassure a small child. "I've heard all I need to hear." Then he turns to the doc and says, "Thank you sir. I won't trouble you again."

And with that, he hauls himself out of the chair, stumbles a bit but pulls himself upright like the soldier he is, and grabs my hand as if he's the one helping me out the door.

All the way home, he held my hand really tight as I fought back tears. It should have been me comforting him, not the other way round.

I admire his spirit though. He's decided to bring a deckchair outside so he can watch me tend our garden. It will always be our garden.

30*th* *June 1941*

I want to make the most of Uncle while he's still with us. I keep thinking about my old teddy bear that Mum and Dad gave me when I arrived in England. I hated that teddy to start with, and I hated them, because they weren't you, Mama. But about a year later, I left the teddy bear on a tram, and never saw it again. I cried buckets for that teddy, feeling guilty and wishing I'd loved it more.

So, I want to hold onto Uncle Harold. I don't want to wake up and find him gone, wishing I'd realised how important he's become to me. I haven't been as kind to him as I might have been—at least, not to start with. I mostly ignored him, apart from folding his newspaper, but that was more about being annoyed with Bess. I just thought of him as an old man. I didn't really give him much thought until he said he'd like to come and help me. Looking back though, he's always been kind. He was the one that helped carry our luggage along the lane, and he gave me my dictionary and thesaurus, which I'll never forget. It's like he could see I was a writer, before I knew it myself. And he lent me books to read, so I could better myself. I haven't ever asked him what he likes to read, and I must. I bet there are lots of people who never got far in school but love books, just like me.

Anyway, I'm trying to make the most of him being down in the garden with me. We sit down with a cup of tea and chat, when I can.

Today, he took a sip then asked me to hold the cup for him. I think even that's becoming difficult—once such a strong man who'd lifted coal on his back and marched with full kit. He sat back in his deckchair and said he had something he needed to tell me.

"Frances, when you came into our lives, I had no idea how much joy you and your little brood would bring me and my Margaret."

He had to pause, holding his chest. He seemed to be fighting for breath, and I feared he might die there and then. I jumped up, but he made a gesture that clearly meant "sit down," so I did. I could see his lips turning blue, but he was determined. He looked up at me, smiling and rubbing his chest as if to say it was just a bit of heartburn, which I knew it wasn't.

"We hadn't seen Stanley for so many years, and we'd no idea what his wife was like, though of course we'd heard about you."

He coughed into his blanket.

"And I confess, when we heard from t'welfare, and then from you to say you were coming, to our shame we were less than keen on a houseful of children. It's been a while since we had several boisterous lads running amok in this house. I know it doesn't put us in a good light, but the only reason we agreed to have you was, we decided it was better to have family than someone else foisted on us that we might not get on with, like, and we'd have no way of persuading to our way of doing things."

He looked down at his clogs.

"I'm sorry," he whispered

I could see regret weighing down on him like a sack of logs for the fire.

"It's OK, Uncle," I said. But his hand came up once more, to stop me in my tracks.

"No. No, don't try and make me feel better, lass. Just hear me out, is all I ask."

I nodded, mollified.

"Thing is, you don't always know a good thing when it comes up and hits you. I know you won't stay forever, especially now t'Blitz is over. You'll have to go home at some point. That's where you belong, after all."

He chuckled, then coughed, and once more fought for his breath, but he shook his hand at me as if to say don't make a fuss, I'll be alright.

"Funny thing is, when you first arrived, I couldn't wait for t'Blitz to be over so you would all go home and leave us in peace. Margaret and I used to talk about it in bed at night, wondering when you'd go back. We saw no advantage in you being here. It was a lot of extra work, or so we thought, and a drain on our finances, especially when Stan's pay stopped and there was no widow's pension to fall back on. But then those kids of yours insisted on giving me a hug and kiss at night, and one night one of them asked me to tell them a story. I told them to leave me alone and go off to bed and behave themselves, but it got me thinking, like. Anyhow, next time they asked, I told them one about a little boy who goes on a train ride and meets a witch and shoves her out o' t'train. God alone knows where that came from, but there was more where it did, and pretty soon they were asking me every night to make up some loony story."

"Yes, I noticed."

I smiled, remembering the persistence of my children and how at their lovely age of innocence, they don't notice hostility. They think everyone's like them and loves being with people, playing. They think adults love making up stories, because I've always done it, Mama, just like you did for me.

"Well, Frances, they melted my heart."

He cleared his throat. Not like someone who's about to choke, but like someone who's trying to make space for the little word soldiers to come out, with all the feelings they carry in their little kit bags. I nodded.

"Eee, and then I saw you working like a trooper, determined to do somat to help us, and you weren't put off by t'mess I'd made of the garden. You got stuck in better'n me, a man."

I could see pain in his eyes. The loss of pride, and something else I couldn't quite put my finger on.

"Which shamed me into helping more. I couldn't but admire you, especially when you took on a paid job and made a go of it. Not any old job, but a respectable one, done by educated people. Which is why I thought you might like my dictionary and thesaurus, to keep like. I know you've insisted you're borrowing 'em, but they're yours."

"But—" I didn't quite know what my objection was, but he interrupted anyway.

"No, no buts, lass," he said, and I knew from his voice there was no point arguing with a dying man.

"Margaret and I are of a mind. You and the children have brought such joy and love and laughter into our lives. I can see why our Stanley chose you as his helpmeet."

And he folded his hands in his lap, lifting them once and placing them down again, as if to say I'm done now.

"Right! Any chance of another cuppa, lass? That's made me reet thirsty!"

Tomorrow when he comes into the garden, I'll ask him what his favourite book of all time is.

1ˢᵗ July 1941

I had a chat to the girls today, Cath and Millie. I always cross the tracks these days when I see them and go to sit on their side of the valley. Uncle H was too ill to come down to the garden, so I still haven't asked him about his favourite book. Anyway, I told them about what he said and about how sad I feel that he's dying. They both gave me a big hug. Silly really, when people are dying all around us, for me to get upset about an old man. It's his time, I know, but I've grown fond of him, and there have been precious few older men in my life. It's made me think how much I miss Dad and what a good man he was. He was a big softie with a voice like dark velvet. Losing him and Mum on the first night of the Blitz, I think everyone was in shock, so my feelings got shoved out of an already overcrowded shelter.

"Frankie," said Cath. "I know this is going to sound crazy, but you know me."

She twirled her finger near her temple, and crossed her eyes, which made all three of us laugh. Then she pulled her face together.

"I once did this thing, after Michael died."

I should stop here, Mama, and explain she was once engaged. Michael was killed in the first week as a bomber pilot. Cath says he was her one and only love, apart from Millie. Anyway, I digress.

"After a few months, I wrote him a letter. Several letters, in fact. I still do write, when there's something I don't want to burden Millie with."

She squeezed Millie's hand.

"Millie's a very good listener. We don't have any secrets."

She gently placed Millie's hand back down on the grass.

182

"Of course, I can never post them, and he will never read them, but it gets it off my chest."

This diary is a bit like her letters, isn't it? But I didn't let on. I just nodded, but my cheeks were on fire. I said I might try writing a letter.

And then their break was over. No doubt I'll see them tomorrow. I'd better decide whether or not I'm going to do this.

2nd *July 1941*

I couldn't sleep, tossing and turning and thinking about what Cath said. It would be strange to write a letter to Uncle Harold when he's still alive. I decided I'd go and keep him company today, when I'd normally be in the garden. I like to get out there every day to keep on top of things, but it'll keep. When I told Maggie I'd like to spend a bit of time with him, she looked delighted.

"Aye, you can be t'one fetching and carrying," she said, in her usual gruff voice.

Uncle Harold has been sleeping in the spare room to give Maggie a good night's sleep. I emptied his potty onto the garden as usual, though there was very little there. I took him up some water just in case he's not been drinking, then I filled the jug and grabbed a rag to wash him. All our flannels have fallen to pieces, but I've cut up an old towel to make some, and stitched hems on. They do the job. As I gaily pulled back the bed clothes, he looked like a little boy who fears being told off.

"I'm sorry, love," he croaked.

The poor man's now incapable of getting out of bed.

I told him not to worry, it wasn't anything I hadn't dealt with before. I went into my best nurse mode. First, I covered him up, then I went to the linen cupboard where luckily, there was one spare sheet. The pillows don't have pillow cases but his wasn't wet or soiled. The blanket was a bit damp, but nothing too bad, so I was able to re-use that. I apologised that he couldn't have a top sheet until I get some washed and dried, but maybe later on today I can make him more comfortable for the night. I rolled him onto his side, propping a rolled-up towel at his back, folded the bottom sheet up to the towel, then I removed the towel and rolled him back as I quickly removed the sheet. Then I washed and dried him, before repeating the rolling exercise to put the new sheet on. His eyes were misty as he reached for my hand, missing several times before he found it and whispered thanks.

I took a cup of tea when I first went up, so I was then able to get on with the washing. Luckily, it's warm and sunny today with a nice breeze, so it should dry.

When I went back upstairs with his breakfast, he was sleeping, so I left it on the bedside table with a fresh cuppa and turned to go. As I reached the door, he whispered:

"Frances. Come and sit wi' me, lass."

So I did. He didn't seem to want to say anything, so I told him I was touched by what he said in the garden, and I said I'm grateful to him and Auntie Mags for welcoming us into their home. That was a white lie—let's face it, Mama, they haven't always been welcoming. I took his hand and told him I've grown very fond of both of them, which is God's truth. He closed his eyes and went to sleep, with a contented look on his face.

Since he was sleeping, I decided to get a bit of scrap paper. Here's what I wrote.

Dear Dad,

When I first came to you at age four, I was scared. I didn't know this strange country, and I wasn't even all that familiar with the language.

Back home, I used to speak Mama's language most of the time. We weren't meant to; we spoke it in secret. Our language and our land were our special place, like a cloak that made us invisible. Mama worked in a big house. We lived in an attic that was too hot in summer and freezing in winter. There was a stern old lady and a younger lady who was married to a handsome but cruel man. I think he might have beaten his wife, but of course she would never have let us see that. She sometimes wore hats that covered her cheeks. But I had eyes like a falcon. I saw something amiss and kept my silence.

I was very good at keeping silence as you discovered when I refused to speak for several months after coming to you. I regret that now. I made you and Mummy suffer. I didn't know your hearts, then. I just knew I had been taken away from Mama because you wanted a girl. Mummy smelled different from Mama, and I didn't want to cuddle her. I now realise that must have hurt her. You both thought you were doing the right thing. You probably believed it to be your Christian duty.

Mama was unmarried and in service. I can now see she had few alternatives. It must have been painful beyond belief to let me go. I suspect the nasty, handsome man, the one that might have beaten his wife, may be my natural father. Not any father to me. You were my real father, Daddy.

I've been staying with my husband's auntie and uncle for several months. Uncle Harold is the second man (apart from Stanley) to make me feel safe. The first was you, Daddy. I eventually learned to trust you. I remember you reading to me, your big strong arms making a secure cradle. It was you who encouraged me to write my own stories, making little books out of scrap paper and string. It was you who sang to me in your dark brown voice and rocked me to sleep despite Mummy saying you were making a rod for your own back. It was you who told me I should stay on at school, if only you could find the money. But I knew that would be a big sacrifice, and in any case, I was headstrong. I wanted to earn a living, so I left school at fourteen like all my friends.

I want you to know you were right. Education sets us free, and I regret now not saying yes and hoping we could somehow find the money, even though I've no idea how that could have been achieved. Despite throwing away my chances when young, I always loved words and, thanks in part to Uncle Harold, I've got better at writing. But I now see what I missed out on. How I would have loved to read more, to immerse myself in stories of other people and places. My road is not an easy one, Dad. It's hard, educating myself. Thanks to Uncle Harold, though, I have a good dictionary and thesaurus, and I'm learning, by devouring his books and the newspaper, how to construct a proper sentence. I'm also helped by the wonderful Sheila Braithwaite, the editor at the newspaper where I work a few hours a week. I love writing, and growing vegetables, more than anything in the world (apart from my children). I remember you in your garden, Daddy. You gave me a little patch when I was a girl, and I learned so much from following you around. Mum used to call me your shadow.

I have to go upstairs to see Uncle Harold, so I will end for now. I need to write to Stan, too. That's going to be difficult.

I love you, Daddy.

Your
Frances. Xxx

3rd *July 1941*

Uncle Harold died early this morning. I was with him most of the day yesterday. Maggie seemed to want to keep busy, and even offered to cook and wash up.

We spent much of the day in companionable silence. He seemed calm—at peace, even. After writing my letter to Dad, I finally asked Uncle Harold which of his books he loved most. That it was Jane Eyre surprised me, given it was written by a woman, from a woman's perspective. The Brontës lived very near here, which might explain some of it. But he said he was drawn to her tenacity, her hard working and her love of reading. He said he could see a lot of Jane Eyre in me.

When the evening came and I put a fresh sheet under his blanket, I could see Uncle Harold's breathing change. He didn't seem to want to wake up when I spoke, though his hand tightened around mine, as if to say I know you're here, lass.

I went down to tell Maggie I thought he was failing, but she said she had some darning to do. So, I went back upstairs. I was determined that man wasn't going to die alone. I must have dozed off sitting upright, because I came to in the wee small hours, aware that the hand I was still holding seemed limp, as if his spirit had already departed. His breathing was laboured, and once again I wondered if I should get Maggie, but I reckoned she was relieved to let me be his midwife into the next world. And so, I sat and watched, and told stories about the trains that go past the bottom of the garden, the unseen spirits that help us work the land, and the huge cabbages we'd produced. Anything, really, just to let him know I was still here and not going anywhere. Somehow, I seemed to get the strength, and I no longer felt tired. It was as if I was being held up by some invisible force. I felt serene, glad to be there.

The birds had started singing, and the light was creeping through the curtains when he seemed to haul himself up a bit in the bed. For a while, I thought he was going to sit up. His chest heaved, and there was a rasping sound, then he slumped back onto his pillow. His ribs moved in and out a few more times but there was no sound, and no energy in his limbs. His chest movements were like a practice for the real business of breathing, except the real thing never came again. When I was sure he'd gone, I placed two pennies on his lids from his trouser pockets, then I said a little prayer, and I thanked him once more for his generosity towards me and my children. Silly to talk to a dead person, but you never know, do you? I pulled the sheet over him, then I went to Maggie, suddenly aware of my heavy limbs.

Maggie instantly woke. As I knelt beside the bed, caressing her hair, she cried:

"Oh no! No! My Harry! What am I going to do without you?"

I held her for a long time, as she sobbed in my arms.

5th July 1941

I went to see my first women's football match today, with Cath and Millie. I felt bad leaving Auntie Mags so soon after Uncle H died, but she insisted. A local mill team was playing against one from Lancashire, near Colne.

I can honestly say I have never seen anything so exciting in my whole life! It's exhilarating, watching women exerting themselves like that, and just for fun! Some of the women had some thigh muscles on them, I can tell you! These days, women are fitter than ever before, what with all that extra exercise. You hear the new land girls complaining, but then they seem to get into their stride and start to relish being in the open air all weathers. I know myself, when I work hard my muscles register a pleasant ache. It doesn't bother me to get dirt in my fingernails. It's clean dirt, as Mum used to say. She had a lot of expressions, including: "You've got to eat a peck of dirt before you die." To which my smart Alec response was: "Is that immediately before, Mum, or does it take a while?"

We were all rooting for our local mill, of course. It was great fun, jumping up and down and shouting—even if I didn't know what I was shouting about! Anyway, our lasses won three nil, which is very respectable. The other side gave them a run for their money though, and there was a lot of pulling of clothing which the referee seemed not to notice or mind, but which caused a great deal of shouting from the touchline.

I might ask my editor whether I can cover the next match.

10ᵗʰ July 1941

It looks as if this house will be either put up for sale or rented out. Maggie's daughter-in-law Iris, who's married to Steve, has said she would like her to live with them. They have quite a big house in Oxenhope. So, it looks as if my decision about whether or not to return to London might be made for me, and I won't be covering any women's football for the paper. And in September, Esther will be off to her new school. I do hope she'll be alright without me to look out for her.

13th *July 1941*

Today was Uncle Harold's funeral. There wasn't a lot of money for flowers or a posh coffin with brass handles. But the vicar did a nice job, and it was surprising how many people turned up to pay their respects.

I met someone he went to school with at Ingrow Primary. It's hard to think of anyone being alive in the last century. Life must have been hard. Apparently, Uncle Harold used to go to school in shoes that had been handed down from one brother to the next. By the time they got to him, the soles were worn through, and you could see his socks poking out. They'd been darned so much there wasn't a lot of sock left, and the shoes were often too small for him. He would go to school all winter like that, in snow and rain and sludge. Plus, he had no coat, so he'd sit there shivering so that when he wrote on his slate, it made a terrible noise, and all the other children in his class would laugh. It's a wonder he made it to adulthood, let alone as old as he was when he died. What a hard life. Mind you, according to this school friend, Uncle H wasn't the only one with no proper shoes and no coat. This is and always has been a poor area, full of mill workers who get paid a pittance.

We sang all the usual hymns—*Abide with me*, and *The day Thou gavest, Lord has ended*, not to mention that most trusty of psalms, 23. It was comforting to sing, and we raised the roof. There was one old gentleman behind me who couldn't sing in tune for toffee. I had to put my hankie over my mouth to stop myself from laughing at the awful din he made. And there was another lady, just a bit older than me I'd say, who had a lovely soprano voice but knew it. You know the type. The I-should-be-a-soloist-in-the-church-choir type. Her voice was louder than anyone else's.

The sermon was lovely. The vicar's a local lad. He said he'd known Harold since his own childhood. Apparently, I'm not the only one that Uncle Harold has helped out with books. When Reverend Clarkson was eleven and had passed his examination for grammar school, his parents were struggling, but they wanted their lad to do well. One day, Uncle Harold overheard them talking about it in the bus station. They happened to mention they needed a particular book—one Uncle Harold had on his shelf. The next day, it appeared on their doorstep, wrapped in newspaper. The reverend said he made it his personal mission to find out who'd done this kind deed, and eventually he tracked Uncle Harold down. But when he knocked on his door, Uncle Harold at first opened it and then when he saw who it was, closed it again. He would never discuss what he'd done or accept any thanks. So, this sermon was the Reverend's way of saying thank you, at last. There wasn't a dry eye in the place, Mama.

20th July 1941

I'm starting to pack, now, not that there's much to pack. I can't seem to motivate myself. I'm walking around the place, picking things up and putting them down again. The veg patch is getting overgrown. I've told the young girl down the road to help herself to whatever she wants. She doesn't look past twenty, with three mouths to feed. Skinny as a rake. I might as well do some good. Maggie seems to have lost the will to do anything for herself. I sometimes catch her talking to herself, or maybe she's talking to Uncle Harold. He was her rock, peg leg or no peg leg. Now he's gone, it's like she's given up, and she's ready to let other people take over. Maybe she'll be better once she's settled into her new home. They're moving her stuff over today. She's sitting in her chair, staring into space as I write. I must steel myself, throw things in cases, book our tickets, and get gone.

I've given the typewriter back to Sheila. I had tears in my eyes as I handed it over. It's become such a friend to me, as has she. I'll miss them both, though I'm hoping to continue writing for the T&A.

I realised yesterday how much the children have grown in a few months. I'm giving a lot of things to other families. I've benefited so much from people's cast-offs; I want to give something back. One wise woman told me when I first came up here and she gave me a load of clothes for the kids, she said:

"It's fine, Frances. You don't have to give anything back to me. It's as if there's this great big pool of giving. You give into it when you can, and you take from it when you need to. So long as you give something to someone when you can, we're square." I've not forgotten that.

It's shoes that are the problem. Their feet grow so fast, and children's shoes are so difficult to get hold of, or at least decent ones. Their poor little feet are squeezing into shoes that either are too small or worn down by their older brothers. I must buy Adam a new pair before we go. I don't want him suffering like poor old Uncle Harold did as a boy.

Dressing Susan is a problem, being the only girl. I've got old dresses the boys wore as babies, but she's growing fast. She's just over four months old now, and ravenous. I've started feeding her bits of mush when I can, like mashed potato and so on. My milk's no longer enough for her. She's sitting up, rolling, and nearly crawling, which should be fun on the train, not to mention the bus or tram.

I've got one last thing to do before we go. I need to write another letter that I cannot send—although I wish I could. This one's to Stan. Here goes.

My darling Stan,

This might be the hardest letter I ever write. Already, the ink is smearing, and I suspect by the time I'm finished, it could be unreadable, but I have my best hanky by me, with my initials in the corner. You remember the one? It was my something new at our wedding, bought and embroidered for me by my now dear departed mum.

Oh, that was a day, wasn't it? With all our parents there, a few friends, and my brother, your sister. We couldn't expect the Yorkshire contingent to make it South, but let me tell you, I've since got to know them very well. You'd be so pleased to see how well I've settled into your family, Stan. Meeting Uncle Harold, even if I couldn't meet your poor old dad, God rest his soul, has given me an insight into you, my love. He was kind and thoughtful like you, and we grew very fond of each other in the short time we had together. But then, this war brings people close. There doesn't seem to be any time to wait and see, does there? When you get to know someone, you don't know whether you'll have them tomorrow, so you make the most of it. Even here in Yorkshire there's a bit of that. Every family has lost someone, if only a friend.

A lot's happened since you went away to sea. At the start, I felt like a fish out of water without you there to make decisions for the whole family. My, how that's changed! It had to. Our daughter is now four months old, Stan. Can you believe that? She's so beautiful. You would adore her, if you could see and hold her. You were always very good with the children. They all wanted you to tell them a bedtime story. Well, that had to be me, once you went—until we went north, and your uncle Harold took over.

Change has become my only constant, Stan. It's time to return to London. But I'm going back a different woman.

I also have to face facts. You won't be coming back to me, will you? Somehow, I have to learn to live without that hope, just as I had to learn a long time ago to live without the hope of ever seeing Mama again, painful though that wound still is.

Goodbye, my love. My one true love. Wherever you are, a big chunk of my heart will always travel with you. As I write, I can see the paper is becoming one big smudge, and I shall have to copy it out again, if necessary, as many times as it takes until I can write these words without an overflowing stream of salty tears.

Goodnight, God bless.

Your ever-loving

Agnes xxxx

21ˢᵗ July 1941

Today, I did something that was long overdue. I asked the boys to sit down, because I had something to tell them.

"Boys, I know we've all been praying each night that God will bring your daddy home safe," I began.

Adam shifted in his chair, looking down. Henry looked at David, and then took hold of his chubby little hand, attempting a smile. Susan played with a rattle I'd made out of an old tin and some beans, bashing on the floor.

"Well, I have some sad news. Daddy won't be coming home—not to Yorkshire, nor to London. You see, Daddy's ship was sunk by the Germans, and since then I haven't heard from him, which isn't like him. I heard from the navy that he's gone to heaven."

I never told them at the time about the sinking. I didn't want to frighten them. Now, I was regretting it. All the words seemed to come out wrong.

"When did his ship sink, Mum?" Adam, looking straight at me, pain oozing out of his face.

"That nice man, George—Dad's friend on the ship—he told me when he came to see me. But I was hopeful, Adam. If George made it onto the rescue ship—your dad was a strong swimmer—I hoped he'd made it too. But I'm afraid he didn't, children."

I never want them to know what he was accused of. When Henry was taunted at school, I made out I didn't know where the rumour had come from. I said it was all lies. I wasn't telling an untruth, exactly. They don't need to know, especially now his name has finally been cleared.

"But can't he come back?" asked little David, his face a picture of fairytale innocence.

"He's with Stephen now, David. They're probably playing football up in heaven, my love. We won't see either of them for a great many years. It's just us now."

"But I want to see him now!"Cried David. Henry pulled him towards his shoulder, tears falling freely from his own eyes. Adam clenched his jaw, then ran upstairs.

25th July 1941

Another sad but proud day at a job well done. I put Esther on the train from Keighley to Leeds. A volunteer was to meet her there and take her to her new school. There are summer boarders whom she will join for the next few weeks. It being a Friday, she's just in time for the weekend, which is more relaxed, though of course she won't start her lessons for several weeks.

Once we'd found the platform and her train, I pulled her to me, smoke enveloping us in a dirty but friendly old blanket. I hugged her so tight I was worried I might crack a few ribs, but she's grown into a sturdy young woman who no longer looks as if she might shatter at any moment into a million tiny fragments that can never be pieced together. She has a quiet strength. She reminds me a bit of me at that age, though I was always more headstrong. But you have to hold yourself up when you've lost your mama. Mamas provide both home ground, and a compass to set you on your way. Mind you, I was always a strange mixture—headstrong, yet timid, always looking round to see what might happen next, and looking to other people to tell me what I should do and where I should go. Esther has a sure footing. She never seems to take a step, even walking to the shops, without having made sure it's the direction she wishes to go in.

After making her collar wet, I held her at arm's length, and said:

"Go well, young lady. You will always have a home with us. You know that, don't you?"

She nodded solemnly, looking up at me through lowered lashes.

"And while we're at it, I just want you to know, I'm enormously proud of you." I swallowed. "And for what it's worth, I've grown to love you. I've never aimed to take your mother's place, even though you very kindly called me Ma from day one. I know that's not the name you used for your real mum. I did the same, once. I had to learn to call a woman Mummy, who wasn't Mama. If your real mother could see you now, and the beautiful—" at this point, she raised her shoulders, inspecting her shoes, so I got hold of her chin and looked into her eyes— "Yes! Beautiful! If your mum could see the beautiful and intelligent young woman she made, I know—" I placed my hand on my heart— "she would be immensely proud of you. Now you'd better get on that train, young lady, before it leaves without you."

She nodded, turned, and climbed onto the train with her little suitcase. I wished I could have sent her off with more. She shut the door, lowered the window, and leaned out. To see her and the other passengers' heads all in a line, you'd have thought you were watching a Busby Berkeley choreography. The whistle blew, and as the train began to pull out, I watched her mouth form the words I longed to hear:

"I love you too, Ma."

It's just as well I had my hankie ready, waving it in my hand until I saw her disappear—just as I saw my Stan disappear, less than a year ago. Once she was out of sight, I blew my nose, hard.

27th July 1941

My widow's pension has come through, backdated. My God, I've never had so much money!

Adam is hardly speaking to me, unless he has to. And Henry's looking upset, whereas David seems to have just got on with the business of playing and being a little boy, once he'd had a good cry. I gave Henry a cuddle as I read to him last night, and he told me he's worried Daddy might get eaten by the fishes, so I had to think on my feet. I didn't want to dwell on what's happening to his body, but then he's not in that body, is he? That thing rotting in the ocean isn't my Stan. He lives on in my memory as the strong, capable rock I leaned on, so I wasn't going to dwell on his salty grave.

"Daddy's not in the sea, silly. He's with Stephen, remember? Stephen needed his daddy, whereas you've got me to cuddle up to. Now little Stephen's got his daddy to cuddle up to, so we're all happy. We've all got someone to take care of us."

Well, not me. I've had to learn to stand on my own two feet, these past months. I went out for fish and chips tonight for me and the kids. Tomorrow, we return to London. I keep shivering despite the warm air. I could hardly eat; the boys finished off my chips.

28th *July 1941*

I stood in the garden that was once my work and my solace, looking all around. Across the tracks, I waved to my memory of Cath and Millie and all the times we shared together, and to the trains that went past the end of our garden, causing great excitement for the children (and probably even more for me).

The dawn tiptoed over the hill like a young woman who's been out all night, shoes in hand so as not to wake her father. I looked at the overgrown cabbages and wondered if they would be picked soon, the potato patch that would hopefully provide food for another family in the coming winter. I stood and stared at the deckchair until I could see Uncle Harold sitting in it, clear as day, his blue-grey eyes twinkling at me as he held out his cup for a refill. I could see his bony knees and his peg leg peeking out from behind the blanket I'd carefully placed over them only minutes before. I wanted to suspend time so I could linger just a while longer, but time was not about to hang about for me. We had a train to catch into Keighley, another to Leeds, and then the overnight to London Kings Cross.

I looked at Adam, who'd come silently to stand by my side, and saw for the first time the young man he's becoming. I'm determined he should go to a good school in London, now he's passed his exams. He's had far better schooling than if we'd stayed in London. He deserves the best possible chance in life. One of my first tasks on our return will be to look at getting him into the grammar school on Blackheath. They were all evacuated, but some staff and pupils are beginning to transfer back to London, thankfully. It'll mean a bus ride every day, but if that means my boy getting a head start, I'm determined to do what I can to ensure it.

I snapped myself together, smiled at him, then took his hand and swished it to and fro as we made our way up to the house, where the other children were all waiting. After all his moods of late, he was very good about me treating him as a little boy who might delight in his mum swinging his hand.

This time, Adam and I were the ones to bear the brunt of carrying the large cases, and Henry managed a smaller one. I got David to push Susan in the pram, even though he could hardly see over the handle. The pram has space at the bottom for all manner of things, which was useful. Of course, there were points at which I had to put my case down and do a bit of pram pushing, then go back for it, but we managed. And so, our little band teetered along the road to wait for the train from Oxenhope. To my surprise when it arrived, Maggie got off it and gave us all a hug, offering to come and see us onto the Leeds train at Keighley.

"I'm not letting you go after all this time without a wave of my handkerchief," she said. I knew resistance was useless.

It's only a couple of stops into Keighley, but of course then we had to change platforms and wait. Maggie sat bolt upright, wearing her summer coat and a feather in her hat as if she was about to go on a day out to Morecambe. When the train began to appear, I felt a stabbing pain in my stomach.

"Well, this is it Auntie. This is where we part company," I said, hurriedly turning to give her a long overdue hug. As I nestled into her shoulder, I whispered: "I shall never forget your kindness, nor Uncle Harold's. You take care of yourself." As we separated, I brushed her shoulder with my hand - as if that could get rid of the salty wetness I'd left there. She didn't flinch, just stood to attention to see us onto the train, her stern face shielding a million words.

"You be good for your Mum, children!" She said as she took her best starched handkerchief out of her handbag.

When the door was shut, I leaned out of the window and blew her a kiss which she waved away, as if to say, "Oh don't be silly now!" Her face was twitching, like it was shutting a lot of tiny doors one after the other, where feelings might otherwise rush out and be seen.

"Don't forget to write, now! I want to hear how Adam gets on at that school you're going to get him into!" she barked. She waved her hankie as the wheels began to crank into action, and I blew her another kiss. I only just caught the last thing she hollered, screwing up her eyes as if the sun was shining right in them on this dreary day:

"You're a very brave lass, young lady! It's like you were one of my own!"

And with that, we were gone from both station and loved ones, whistles blaring and smoke drawing a curtain between us.

30th July 1941

Today, one of the first things I did was to visit the pawnbroker. I wasn't sure if my ring would still be there after more than six months. I searched the window and saw so many rings. So many women's heartbreak. There was a lovely emerald, a tiny sapphire, and a ruby. Lots of diamond solitaires, most much bigger than Stan could ever have afforded. But I couldn't see my ring. Eventually, I pulled myself together and went in.

The pawnbroker recognised me.

"Hello, Mrs. Cockroft! And what have you for me today?" He carried on polishing a silver bracelet with his soft cloth.

"Oh. Oh, no, sorry. No. I haven't come to pawn anything, Mr. Simmonds. I've come to see if you happen still to have my diamond ring."

I could feel my palms go moist, my throat dry.

"Actually, yes. We do still have it. I put it by last week for a gentleman in uniform, but I suspect he must have been called back to ship earlier than he anticipated. So yes, it's still here. Just give me a moment." He carefully placed down both cloth and bracelet.

At the mention of a naval man, I had to hold onto the counter. I watched him disappear into the back room and listened to him shifting step ladders and rustling boxes. Finally, he reappeared, my ring in his hand, and my stomach did a little somersault.

But he wasn't handing it over so quickly. He adopted a concerned voice as he announced how much money was owed. But I'd done my sums. I had coins to spare as I counted them out into his palm, along with some nice crisp bank notes.

I must have lost a bit of weight because the ring's looser on my finger. But it's been cleaned up, so it looks good as new. I shan't be taking it off in a hurry.

2nd *August 1941*

A complete surprise in the post today. I received a packet from the MOD with a Military Cross in it acknowledging Stan's service. I wasn't expecting that. The tears are never far away, what with having my ring back, and now this.

4th August 1941

I went to see the headmaster at the boys' school on the heath today. I wrote to him the day after we arrived, and a reply came on Saturday asking me to come today, Monday, at 10 a.m. He has a plush office, and a Scottish accent that makes him seem slightly haughty. What with me never having even been to secondary school, let alone grammar school, I felt myself to be on the back foot, but I could hear Hilda's voice inside my head telling me we're all equal in the eyes of God. Quakers, in the olden days (sixteen hundred and something), got into trouble for not doffing their hats to powerful people. They don't even use Mr. and Mrs., or Doctor. Just plain first and second names. No one is better than anyone else, Hilda says. Not even the King. When she first told me I said I thought you could go to prison for that kind of attitude. To which, she said it wouldn't be the first time. I didn't like to inquire further, but she said Quakers have often gone to prison for their beliefs. This George Fox, who started Quakers, was in prison several times. Even women went to prison.

Anyway, I sat listening to this man drone on about how special his school is, trying not to fall asleep, when he said:

"You do realise, Mrs. Cockroft, our boys are among the finest in London." Statement, not question. "It will be imperative, if we accept your son—er—"

"Adam. Adam Cockroft."

"Yes," he looked at me, his head tilting to one side. "Adam."

"His father served King and Country. I have his medal here to prove it. And if you're worried about whether Adam will come dressed correctly, let me assure you I not only have a widow's pension, but a

private income. I earn a living as a journalist, and I own my own house."
I enjoyed that, even if my cheeks did go hot as I said it.

"I see!" Mr. McArthur's chin disappeared into his neck as he peered over his specs, his mouth pulled into the kind of shape you might make if you'd just stepped in some dog muck.

"And he will have every support from me," I said, looking directly into his eyes.

Where did I learn to be so brave talking to the likes of him? Is this the same Aggie who thought teachers were all superior to her?

He fiddled with some papers on his desk as he muttered almost to himself:

"Well, his results are very good. One hundred per cent on the intelligence test. And over ninety on both English and Mathematics." I saw his jaw set as he oh-so-slowly turned towards me.

"I will be in touch with the term dates and a list of uniform, Mrs. Cockroft."

He held out his hand for me to shake, then removed it almost as soon as we touched, changing the shape of his hand as he extended it towards the door.

I walked out with a fire in my belly. I won't allow him to put me down again. I'll show him.

7th August 1941

The uniform list came through the post today. First, I visited the Woolwich Equitable to draw out some money, then I took Adam to Cuffs, the department store, to get him kitted out. Thank God for double coupons for children. Less than a month until he starts his new school.

While I was in Woolwich I bumped into my old friend Shirley. She's in the family way again, due sometime in January. She looked all sheepish when she saw me, no doubt thinking of Stephen, so I got hold of her hand and told her I'm delighted for her. Her shoulders relaxed, and she let out a long breath. Then she hugged me tight and told me she was really glad to see me back. That made me feel all warm inside.

9th August 1941

I sat down with a pencil and a bit of paper and worked out how much I have in my savings account, what I need to spend before I next get paid, and what I have spare.

And then, I went shopping. It being a Saturday, Adam looked out for the other three.

I lugged my very own typewriter home from Woolwich today! My goodness, it was difficult. After I got off the bus at the Links, I had to stop several times. I was glad I didn't have any other shopping. Now it sits on the table, gleaming. I already had paper and carbon, so I can now start submitting really professional looking articles. I typed a letter to Sheila Braithwaite to show her how good it looks. As I pushed the carriage return, it moved along smoothly, with a satisfying bicycle bell "ping" at the end. And the keys never get stuck! I feel like the cat that got the cream.

15th August 1941

I covered my first women's football match today, as a journalist! I got a front row spot and all! Just like last time, it was so exciting I was glad I was standing. I was torn between scribbling notes and waving my hands like a lunatic!

The match was between two very good teams: A.V. Roe, who make Lancaster bombers, and Fairey Aviation Company, another aircraft manufacturer based in Hayes, Middlesex. Interestingly, A.V. Roe also has a factory in Yorkshire. Needless to say, muggins had to travel over to Hayes, which took most of the day. Adam sorted out the troops with a bit of spam and bread and marge until I could get in and give them eggs on toast. I'm shattered. Now, I have to write it up, but that will be a treat, on my own typewriter! I would say thank goodness it's the weekend, but anyone with children knows that is no break at all, Mama.

22nd August 1941

I've spent the whole of this week getting everything ready for Adam to start his new school in just over a week. I don't like to leave things to the last minute. He's got an ironed shirt, shorts, clean socks and underwear, plus his school blazer and cap. Then he's got his very posh briefcase bought in the market. I love that smell of new leather. Inside is a pencil, rubber, sharpener, protractor, compass, set square, and ruler, all in a nice wooden box with sliding lid. I've also had to buy exercise books for maths and English, and a book on grammar bought direct from the school. I think I feel more nervous than he does.

1ˢᵗ September 1941

Adam wouldn't let me accompany him on the bus to Blackheath. He wouldn't even let me go to the bus stop.

"I'm big and ugly enough, you always say Mum."

I took one look at him in his new uniform and saw a different boy to the one I gave birth to more than eleven years ago. I could see it was time to let him make his own mistakes, though I've a feeling there won't be many. He's a sensible lad with a head on him like his dad's, which made me feel secure for many years.

I came home to a lovely letter from Esther, full of news about her dormitory and the routine there during the summer vacation, as well as one or two snippets about the girls she's met, and what food they get to eat. She said her tummy's more settled these days; I'm greatly relieved. She didn't mention how she's sleeping. It sounds wonderful, though. All *What Katy did at school.* I wish I'd had such opportunities, but I don't begrudge her any of it. She's been learning to sail on a nearby lake and taking healthy walks. She's joined a choir and is learning chess—one of the girls is teaching her and says she's a natural. It was lovely to hear how she's settling in. Replying will give me something to do in the evenings, when I miss her company. I would let Adam stay up a bit later, but now he's at grammar school I want him to get plenty of sleep. Next year, who knows? Maybe his brother will join him. Henry's bright enough, even if he is more like me—keener on climbing trees than learning his lessons. David seems to have the best of both in him. He's funny, creative—he loves to draw—and he's really good at mental arithmetic. He's made new friends here really quickly, as well as picking up on old friendships—which surprised me, for one so young. I didn't think he would remember anyone.

I'm worried about Hilda, though. She's very thin, and her skin looks sallow, as if she had jaundice. I'm not sure whether to come out with it and ask her what's up. Maybe I'm afraid of what I might find out.

*3ʳᵈ **September 1941***

Two years since this awful war began. Last night I went on one my travels; it's been quite a long time. I was once again with our ancestors, Mama.

They summon me, wordlessly, to the top of our sacred hill. I can see the snow on the mountains opposite, but there is a hint of warmth on my skin as I climb that familiar, blessed place. When I reach the top, I can see both the lake and river, weaving its way through whatever cracks it can find in the mountains.

Our ancestors appear with traditional facial tattoos, spears, and shields. They wear either blankets or feathered cloaks draped around their bodies.

A man and a woman step forward to greet me. Their eyes are like dark gemstones, shining in the low light, and they each have a feather in their hair.

They don't speak, at least not in words. As they take a step towards me, I'm overcome by a strong energy. It's as if they're transmitting something to me. I "hear-feel" them say they're passing some important work on to me. They say I'm in the right place; I was meant to return to London. My work is in my writing and in raising my children well, including Esther, my foster daughter. These are my tasks.

It's as if, despite them not touching me, they've attached an electric cable to the top of my head, sending shock waves throughout my body and creating a kaleidoscope of rich, vibrant colours!

When my vision recovers they're gone, and I begin my slow descent. The first flowers of spring are emerging. With each step down the hill I feel myself falling through time and space, back into this body, my bed, and my daily life.

When I woke, I felt a clarity I haven't experienced for a long time, and a sense of purpose. The first thing I did, after getting ready to start the day, was go into the garden here and start digging.

213

5th September 1941

I took the bull by the horns today. It's less than a year since I met Hilda, and yet even though I've spent several of those months away from her, I feel as if I've known her forever. I care for her as if she were my sister.

There were just the two of us embroidering banners upstairs in the Links when I noticed her drop her needle and touch her stomach. Knowing as a Quaker she's one for plain speaking, I asked her straight:

"Hilda, you're sick, aren't you?" I rested my own work in my lap, so she knew I wasn't going to let it go.

"Yes," was all she said, and took up her needle.

I reached out and took the embroidery off her, accidentally pricking her finger as I did so. She graciously sucked at it without a word. It's nothing we haven't all done to ourselves a million times, but I felt bad that I'd hurt her. She looked up from her work, looking for all the world like a little girl who'd spilled the family's precious milk, full of remorse.

"Hilda, tell me," I said, my voice softened. Don't ask me how, but I understood in that moment—her greatest fear is not being able to serve others. No physical pain is quite as bad as feeling you've let people down.

"I didn't want to tell you. You've got enough on your plate," was her predictable reply. Same old Hilda, always thinking of others before herself. I waited, willing her to let me be there for her, for once.

"I'm afraid I have cancer."

She might as well have been telling me her cake hadn't risen by the tone of her voice, but her body told a different tale. I waited again. She coughed.

"It seems I haven't long, so I've just decided to carry on as normal. That's the best thing for it." She couldn't look me in the eye.

"Where?" I asked, my voice so thin I wasn't sure she'd heard me.

"Where? Oh, in my tummy somewhere. Now, can I have my embroidery back, please?"

I knew it was useless to pursue the topic, and so I handed her both needle and embroidery. We continued in silence, my eyes stinging so much I stabbed myself a couple of times.

7th September 1941

It's strange, being mistress in my own house. On the one hand, I have everything to do and no one to share the chores with, but on the other hand, I decide when to scrub my steps and when to let them stay as they are so that I can get on with my writing or go and meet my friends at the Links. My days are full. Now we're back in London, they go something like this:

Monday is washing day, as always, and that takes up most of the day, so Monday evening's tea is a simple affair like spam fritters, with maybe semolina for afters. I love my wireless. I even enjoy polishing it. The smell of lavender polish is strangely reassuring, Mama. I listen to the home service while I'm still busy, so I can update myself on what's happening war-wise. By the time I've washed up, I'm nearly ready for bed but I do like to sit and listen to the light programme, for a bit of relief. They play lovely songs, like "We'll meet again," and "The white cliffs of Dover." I can just imagine our troops listening to that and thinking of home—especially the navy lads. I always get a dull pain in my chest when I hear it, thinking of Stan. They sometimes play oldies, like "I'll be with you in apple blossom time." I love the Glenn Miller tunes, though. They make me feel like dancing. Once I've done a bit of sewing or knitting listening to the light programme and had a cup of tea, I can go off to bed happy.

On Tuesdays, I still don't iron everything, but I do iron Adam's shirts. He has to look the part. Then I get out in the garden and work hard physically, whatever the weather. I don't get as much time to see my friends at the Links as I used to, though sometimes I get help from them with digging, on the promise of some veg when it all starts coming up. This time of year, you'd think there isn't much to plant, but I'm starting off the spring greens, broad beans, winter cabbages, peas, onions, and that old standby for soups and stews, turnips. I usually have to do some shopping at some point on a Tuesday just like every other weekday, and I make something like a meat and potato pie (and a fruit one for afters—no point in wasting pastry!).

Wednesday is more of the same, but maybe less time in the garden so I can get on with my writing. I work straight onto my typewriter, always making a carbon copy. Tea is usually something like sausage and mash, and tinned fruit with custard for afters—though of course the milk is often running low so I make it fairly weak, as in fact I do all the milk puddings. Evaporated milk is a great stand by.

Thursday is when I have a real push on my writing, but I also have to do some housework, which breaks up the day. Tea is something like shepherd's pie, or maybe meat pudding, and spotted dick.

Friday is when I dash my copy off to the editor. Tea is always fish, and afters is usually a crumble with custard.

On Saturday, I whizz through the house, and I make sure I'm on top of what the kids need for Monday (more washing, drying, and ironing!). I give them a sandwich for lunch that day and we have our main meal in the evening: usually egg and chips, with bread and butter pud for afters. The kids love that.

Sunday is precious family time. I learned from my parents that the best things in life are free, so we usually walk up to the park and maybe into Jack Woods, Castle Woods and Oxleas Woods. There are lots of bomb craters along the way, of course—especially in the woods at the back of our house. It's scary thinking about how close those bombs got every night, and how lucky we were to survive being bombed out. Not everyone was as fortunate.

The Sunday walk always happens after a roast, if I can get the meat.

If not, maybe toad in the hole. I make up for the small meat portions with loads of roasties, and I make Yorkshire puddings with egg, flour and water. Lots of veg, which I hope will soon be home grown once more. Afters is something like treacle tart. Tea is a nice bit of bread and dripping round the fire. Pure gold.

So, I've got it all organised, though I wish I could see more of my friends. I usually bump into Shirley at least once a week, and sometimes she pops round for a cuppa. But busy is good, and the money from my work for the Telegraph and Argus comes in handy.

9th *September 1941*

I decided I'd better get Susan christened, Mama. I'm going to see the vicar on Sunday. I can't have her little soul wandering around purgatory if something awful happens to her, which God forbid it ever does.

14ᵗʰ September 1941

I had a word with the vicar, and I've got it all booked in. The christening is set for April 11, 1942—a Saturday. Apparently, they've had a bit of a rush on. Now, I need godparents. It's not difficult to find godmothers—I'll ask Shirley, and I'll have a think about finding a second one, but these days, apart from Shirley, my friends are a Quaker, a Catholic, and a Jew, none of whom would quite fit the bill.

Susan is taking to her solids like a duck to water. I give her a bit of mashed potato on a teaspoon for her dinner and tea, and then at tea time, when I make the main meal for the boys, I usually give her a bit of whatever milk pudding I've made. For breakfast, she gets a bit of the boys' porridge. The first time I tried her, she stuck her little pink tongue out and licked at it, just like they all do, but now she knows what's coming and opens her mouth.

Of course, she still gets plenty of me, too! I love those feeds—a bit of quiet time when I have to sit down, otherwise she wouldn't feed. I must make the most of these days. I'm already giving her a bit of cold, milky tea in a bottle.

16ᵗʰ September 1941

I wasted no time in speaking with Shirley, and she was delighted to be asked to be Susan's godmother, Mama. In fact, she was quite touched. Stan found the godparents for the boys. It wasn't seen as my department, given they were his sons.

I could ask David's wife, Brenda, to be the other godmother. We don't see a lot of each other, but we've always got on well. They seem reluctant to visit London, but I daresay they'd come for that. But who can I ask to be her godfather? David's already godfather to my David.

219

21st September 1941

I never seem to have time to turn round these days, let alone write to you, Mama. I'm trying to keep up with my correspondence in the evenings when the children are in bed, my chores are done, I've written my weekly article, and my muscles and eyelids are so heavy I could just drop. But I know how precious letters can be. Esther and I have settled into a weekly letter each. We overlap, so I tend to answer what she said in the last but one she sent, but it seems to work well. She's getting to grips with maths I've never heard of. I wish I had her knowledge. She's also being taught grammar, whereas I have had to learn the hard way, and I still don't always get it right. But she loves her reading best and is often to be found in a corner of the garden, her head in a book like *Wuthering Heights*, *The Mill on the Floss*, or of course the perennial *Jane Eyre*. Those are all books I've read and loved, so we're able to discuss the characters, which bits we cried over and so on. I'm so grateful she came into my life.

1st October 1941

Every time I see Hilda she seems a little thinner. She keeps her serene smile at all times, but she looks like death warmed up.

She doesn't always come round to the Links now when Ruth, Sandhya, and I are there. We continue the work as best we can, but of course this country doesn't want to hear a peace message, so wedded are they to Churchill and war. Who can blame them, with husbands and sons at sea, being shot at in the air, or being blown up in Africa? Every week, I hear of another woman widowed or losing a son. I channel it all into my writing.

Shirley came round for a cuppa the other day, and whether it's because I asked her to be godmother or what I don't know, but as she left, she gave me a big hug and told me she was glad we've remained friends all these years. I didn't know where to put myself.

Some of us have started a communal allotment, which works better than me trying to grow veg all on my own in the back garden. There's some land out the back that isn't occupied, so we've turned it to good use. It's cheery, having a chat as we all dig. I've created a run for my chickens, and I'm growing veg there as well as in the garden. Of course, there is not as much to be grown over winter, but we have cabbages and Brussels sprouts, parsnips, and potatoes. I grow cress indoors on blotting paper all year round. The children get involved in that. I have a goat in the garden, though she's not my best friend right now, having chewed some of the baby's things that fell off the line the other day. You have to be so careful!

I get little time these days to come and see you, Mama, or to travel anywhere else for that matter. But I'm content. I only seem to go on my travels when I'm not at ease in myself. It seems to sort me out when I do. It sometimes hurts, like a dislocated shoulder slotting back into place, but the relief can be immense. At other times, it leaves me sad, but less so these days.

15th October 1941

The allotment is proving a good way to feel more at home here. Even though it was my home before I went away, I went a married woman with no income or work of her own, and I came back a homeowner, a widow, and someone who can provide for herself and her children. I think some people round here who knew me only as Mrs. Cockroft—neighbours, that is, rather than people I would count as friends—may have thought I was acting a bit above my station when I came back. But working the land together means they now see me getting dirty, not afraid of a bit of hard graft, laughing and joking with the best of them. It's done far more for this neighbourhood than simply putting food on the table, Mama.

Esther only tells me the happy things in her letters, but I make sure she knows I'm thinking of her. I asked how well she's sleeping, and she replied fine, on the whole. I bet she still has those nightmares. Being away from us will give her time to reflect on what happened.

The children and I have settled into a new routine, being just us. For months now, I've had to assert my authority where previously I could say, "you just wait until your father gets home!" Now, it's all down to me. I have to be mother and father to those children, and the boys can be a handful—especially Henry. He's old enough to answer back, and not young enough to hide in my skirts anymore. We've been to visit the grammar school. Next year, God willing, he will join his brother.

6th November 1941

Hilda's weakening. I've been keeping an eye on her, which is why I've not written in a while. I spend most mornings there now, holding her hand and making cups of tea or whatever I can persuade her to swallow. She's skin and bone, frequently vomits up what I give her, or has to rush to the loo—well, her potty. The times when she doesn't make it have become more frequent, so I wash sheets and attempt to dry them round her tiny bedroom fire. Seeing her try to get up after using the potty is torture, so I give her a hand. I can feel the bones in her arm. At times, I have to lay her on the bare mattress with just a rough blanket over her. I feel bad for doing that, but she remains stoical and apologetic for bothering me.

The three of us take shifts: Ruth takes over from me, then Sandhya takes over from her and stays the night. Such a dear soul. It's a shame she and her fella never managed to have kids before he was called up. But then, look at Hilda. At least she won't leave any little ones behind. God forgive me for thinking that, but not having kids can be a blessing at times like this.

I may be finding it hard to make time to write this diary, let alone the work I get paid for, but I feel privileged to be able to care for my friend in her hour of need.

Yesterday morning, I sat with Hilda as usual. Their house doesn't have a trace of Christmas in it. They don't believe in celebrating it, which is just as well this year.

The smell of sickness leaped at my nostrils as I entered the room. I was relieving Sandhya, and she looked worn out. She usually gets a bit of sleep, but she said Hilda had been sick a lot in the night. I could see traces of blood in the bucket. I set about getting towels, rags, and hot water to clean her up. I could tell she was grateful, even though she winced every time I tried to move her.

By the time I was done, she was obviously exhausted and shut her eyes. I took up my knitting, enjoying the peace and the pleasant smell of fresh linen and soap.

"Aggie," she said. "I get a feeling you're burdened with a secret. Now would be a good time to unburden yourself."

You could have knocked me down with a feather. How the heck did she know? But while Susan took a nap in her pram, I began to talk, very matter-of-fact:

"I spent the first few years of my life in Aotearoa, Hilda. It's what you call New Zealand. Before I came here, my name was Ahurewa. Mama and I lived in a big house where she worked, in a town called Queenstown—my people called it Tāhuna. My language was Te Reo Māori, when I was little. I was taken from my Mama, aged four, and adopted by a British couple—Mum and Dad."

I've never told a soul so many details before, not even Stan. I told Hilda I can't remember many of the old words or phrases you used to say to me, which hurts. But I remember what you whispered as they pulled me from you, my fingers desperately clinging to your dress until the man prized them off. I don't know how to write it, but I do know its meaning: "I will call your name on the wind." You also mouthed it as I reached the door, your eyes betraying your own pain at parting. I listened, waiting for your voice on the wind. I knew you never told a lie.

The day I landed in England was also the day the First World War was declared—I sometimes think it's my fault that this one started. I thought I must be jinxed. I was given three new English names—Frances Agnes Drake. I told all this to Hilda.

"They carted me off to church within a week, to make it official. The vicar wore a dress and poured water on me, which despite the hot day did not go down well with me. I wanted to punch him."

I felt a bit shame-faced, what with Hilda being a Quaker and against violence. But I felt compelled to tell her everything, so I carried on. I needed to.

"After that, I had to go every Sunday, until I married Stan."

I told Hilda how I continued to listen for you, Mama:

"For a whole year I waited, whenever there was a wind, to hear Mama calling my name. In my four-year-old head, when she called, I would be sucked back along the wind and across the earth, to where I belonged. But as I strained to hear her voice, all I heard was English birdsong, so different from the Tūi, and the rustle of the wind in the trees. And then it dawned on me. Mummy and Daddy had changed my name from Ahurewa to Frances because they loved a Saint Francis. I decided the reason I couldn't hear her was that she was calling someone who no longer existed. Eventually, I started talking English with as good a London accent as everyone else. Everyone round here either went to school with me or has known me for years. They seem not to care that I look "Celtic," so long as I sound like them and behave like them. Now, I have to strain to remember the words my Mama and I spoke together in our sacred, special times within the sanctuary of our room."

I shivered, despite the fire in the grate. I told her I always used to look to other people to make me feel safe and secure, how much I miss my adoptive parents and my Stanley. Then I told her what it was like going north, missing home all over again, how I missed her and Ruth and Sandhya, how it was so foreign at first.

I glossed over my achievements since then. I didn't want to boast, not even to a dying woman. But I did say that, despite my nervousness and uncertainty about whether I could manage alone, I found some strength from somewhere.

I spoke of how I won over Uncle Harold and Auntie Mags, and how I've cared for and come to love that little angel from heaven, Esther.

Eventually, I even told her—since I was getting things off my chest—about my little travels, and how sometimes when I go on them I see things that turn out to be true.

When I'd finished, I took a big gulp of cold tea and carried on knitting. I glanced over at Hilda, who still seemed to be sleeping peacefully, her breathing nice and regular, so I went back into my own little world. But I was jolted out of it.

"You have done exactly what God wanted of you, Agnes."

Hilda's voice sounded like sandpaper, painfully scraping over some old painted woodwork—but she had more to say.

"You have become your own woman. All you need to do now is believe it, and believe you are doing precisely what God wants from you."

Then she stopped. I thought she'd finished, but she seemed to gather every ounce of energy for the next bit:

"The world is your oyster. Just never forget we are all equal in the eyes of the Lord."

Her head and shoulders dropped back into the bed. I could see her lips were dry, so I held a cup to them, but she shook her head with what little strength she had left.

When Ruth appeared at the door, I was both relieved to see her and dismayed; this meant it was time for me to go home and cook—to enter a different world, where life goes on regardless. I must have looked pathetic, because Ruth put her hand on my shoulder, and softly said:

"It's OK Aggie. I'm here now, and you have other things to do."

"But what if —" I began, not wanting to complete the sentence.

"All shall be well," was all she would say. And so, I left.

Around tea-time, Ruth and Sandhya came to my door. The boys had just got home from school. I knew when I saw them on my top step that Hilda had left her suffering behind.

20ᵗʰ November 1941

Today is my thirty-second birthday and would have been my twelfth wedding anniversary. The Quaker funeral and burial was held at Blackheath Meeting House. Never having been to a Quaker funeral before, I hadn't a clue what to expect, but I think they're used to a lot of non-Quakers attending these things. Someone stood up and gave a quick overview of what would happen; it's not like a church funeral. They called it a Meeting for Worship in Thanksgiving for the Grace of God, as shown in the life of Hilda Fairclough. There was no singing of hymns, no sermon, not even prayers. Most of the time we were in the Meeting House, everyone sat in silence. I looked around, waiting for something to happen, then decided to make the most of the peace. To be honest, I found it to be very religious in a sort of non-religious way. A bit like when we used to climb up Te Tapu-nui, Mama, and look down over Lake Wakatipu. A sense of being close to God. I began to see swirling colours behind my eyes, moving towards me like water going down a drain, getting bigger as they did so, then as soon as the colours filled my vision, a new spiral began approaching from the far distance. Beautiful, vibrant colours with lots of purple, blue, violet and green—the clearest apple green that made me feel contentment in my chest.

Several lovely things were said about Hilda, puncturing my reverie as if someone had dropped a heavy book in a library—yet somehow, I still felt serene as I listened. One woman mentioned how welcoming Hilda had been when she first started attending, another that Hilda had served as an elder and overseer (whatever that means) and been instrumental in ensuring the Meeting continued to flourish during these difficult times of war. And of course, her work with the Kindertransport was mentioned. I would have liked to speak up at that point, but my voice wouldn't come out of its hiding place.

The most moving ministry was from her husband, Paul. Given compassionate leave from the FAU, his eyes were puffy and red. I could see him shifting in his seat for some time before he stood. But his voice was clear and strong as he spoke. To my shock, he mentioned that it wasn't their gift to have children, but God had other plans for her. He spoke with feeling about what a kind, good woman she was, and how many people in the Meeting had sought her out for advice and guidance in times of trouble. He held onto his hat, twiddling it round in his hands as he said haltingly that he would miss her kindness, her gentleness, and her shining example of God's love.

After the Meeting for Worship, we went out to the burial ground so that the casket—a simple wooden affair without any brass—was lowered into the ground. Apparently, she will have no headstone, but a record will be kept. Almost no one cried openly, though there was much dabbing at eyes. Certainly, no wailing.

And so, we are three. This strong but motley crew of women who've supported each other through thick and thin now stands with a gaping hole in its side, to let in all manner of winds and rain. I fear we'll never entirely recover our form. There will forever be a weak place where once she stood, quiet but immovable.

24ᵗʰ November 1941

As if she knew how much I need her right now, I've heard from Cath on behalf of her and Millie. Here's what she wrote:

Dearest Frankie,

We miss you so much! Are you sure you don't want to offload those delightful children of yours and run off to join the land army in Keighley? We could do with you, especially on these cold, dark, and wintery days. What's it like down your way? I bet you have subtropical temperatures and are always out dancing. We miss you at our dances. They aren't the same without being able to throw you about and whisk you around the floor. Millie was positively jealous of you when she saw you could actually put one foot in front of the other, but she's got over it because she loves you just as much as I do.

Did I ever tell you I actually enjoy getting my hands dirty? You should see the muscles on me now! Those weedy servicemen have got nothing on me! I'm never happier than when I've got my dungarees on.

Anyway, do write and tell us all your news. Millie says hello. Her writing isn't as good as mine, so she has given me this pleasure.

Big hugs,
Yours forever,
Cath

I couldn't stop smiling. I might not have Hilda anymore, but I have a land army of strong, loving women marching right behind me.

26th November 1941

Blimey, these letters are coming thick and fast. The latest one, from Auntie Mags, wasn't nearly as much fun to read as the one from Cath, but it was lovely to know she's settling in with her daughter-in-law and making herself useful with the little ones. She said it's good being a Grandma, though why she didn't already know, that I've no idea. She said she hadn't realised how much joy the little loves bring. I suppose she must have previously always been too busy and tired to bother with them. She sent her letter in a Christmas card made by one of the children, with a picture of Santa Claus on the front.

If only I could get a letter from My Stan—though I know, of course, that's impossible—or one from you, Mama. That would burst my heart wide open.

Nearly a year since my darling Stephen died in my arms. So much has happened. So much that he missed. He will never know what it is to go to secondary school like his big brothers all hopefully will. He'll never bring a girl home. I will never see him married and happy. It still feels like a big, wind-blown hole in my heart. I won't be able to write for a bit, I suspect, as the anniversary hits home and the world keeps spinning, the war keeps raging just as before.

8th December 1941

I can hardly believe Christmas is coming round so fast, and this terrible war has been going now for over two and a quarter years. I wonder how much longer? Yesterday, the Japanese bombed somewhere called Pearl Harbour, which is in Hawaii—American territory. And so, they join us.

10th December 1941

Mama, I went on one of my journeys last night, except it was a bit different.

I was sitting in my armchair in the evening, knitting a new jumper for Adam. I must have shut my eyes for five minutes, and before I knew it, I found myself by Lake Wakatipu, sitting on a rock.

Next to me sits Hilda. I'm pleased to see her. It doesn't seem strange, or scary, or out of the ordinary that she's here, in Aotearoa. Then, from behind her, Stephen emerges. It's as if Hilda has been holding him back, as a special treat for me. He runs to me, burying his head in my chest. I wrap my arms around him, enjoying the feel of his closeness, and tears come, unbidden. I don't want this moment to end. Even as I focus on the present, though, I'm aware it cannot last. I hold on tenaciously, to the moment, and to him.

It occurs to me to ask why I'm seeing Hilda in Tāhuna (Queenstown as she would know it), not London, and why Stephen is with her—but I know I don't need to. She seems to envelop me with her soft presence, as she half-whispers, half-sings:

"Here is where one of your hearts resides, Ahurewa."

The same tears flowed as I returned, leaving behind these souls that once I walked alongside. It didn't strike me as odd until later, that she had used my birth name, but I understood that I live with two hearts—one in England, and one in Aotearoa. In fact, I probably have three now—one in the north of England, one in London, and one in Queenstown. Home is where the heart is, after all, and I have grown to love three homes, with a name in each—Ahurewa in Tāhuna, Aggie in London, and Frankie in the West Riding.

15th December 1941

Last night I had to go to a parents' evening at Adam's school. Luckily, I didn't have to take Henry and David with me because Esther is home from school—they finish a bit before the children in the local grammar schools. She looks well and has even put on a bit of weight.

I'm as pleased as punch. Our Adam is doing exceptionally well. His form teacher told me he's so polite and well-spoken, and his English teacher says his spelling and grammar are excellent. Plus, he has a flair for a story. I wonder where he gets that from? Even his maths and science teachers were pleased with him. I walked out of there with my head held high, clutching Adam's hand. I caught the headmaster's eye as I left, and he positively beamed at me. Ha! I suspect one day that man will be glad I brought my son to his school.

Chanukah also started last night, and tonight Ruth has asked if Esther could go round. It must be hard for her, with Nathan being a POW. I'm sure Esther will be a great comfort. It'll help them both.

20th December 1941

Susan now eats almost the same as her brothers, but much smaller portions and of course well mashed up. She's such a good little girl, Mama.

She still feeds from me in the morning as soon as she wakes up, then has another in the middle of the day, and one before bed. That's all. The rest of the time, she eats her food and has a bit of cold tea in her bottle. If she's hungry between meals, I give her a bit of cold porridge, or mashed potato. She's a bonnie baby, and everyone says so. She's beginning to crawl, though she's at that distressing stage for babies of meaning to go forwards but going backwards instead. It's torture watching them go through that. Still, she'll be into my knitting soon enough, unravelling what I've been making I've no doubt!

The boys are now off school for the Christmas break, and of course we have Esther with us too, so I have a house full. The boys, thankfully, all love to play out in the woods at the back of the house in all weathers and know to keep clear of the allotments so as not to disturb our labours. Esther is happy to help me, and to read quietly. She loves Susan and spends hours playing "Round and round the garden" with her, to delighted giggles. You'd think they were sisters—which I suppose they are.

It's good to have such young life in the house, amidst all this death and destruction.

I can't say I'm looking forward to another Christmas without Stan, the first of my new life in this house as a widowed mother, but I'll put on a good show of it, for the sake of the children.

28th December 1941

Christmas was a fairly dull affair, though I did make sure Esther's birthday was celebrated this time. I bought her a copy of *The Secret Garden*, by Frances Hodgson Burnett. I remember finding it at the library when I was about her age, indulging in my fantasies about a walled garden just for me. It's a book to get lost in, to hide in, to rest in. She also spent some time with Ruth and her children, though of course Ruth is pretty downhearted right now. In fact, Chanukah isn't a big festival for Jewish people. The one they have near Easter, the Passover, is much bigger apparently, but this year of course we were in Yorkshire. There are lots of Jewish holidays; I don't know them all. They have a different New Year from us. Theirs is in September, and they count the years differently, which isn't surprising since we take ours from the birth of Christ.

I missed having any other family to share the festive season with, and of course with rationing it was hard to find things to give as presents. I got them each a small item of clothing with the coupons I'd saved up, and I went to a toymaker in the hollow and bought a wooden toy for Susan: a pull along train, which she loves even if she can't yet walk. The boys were more difficult to buy for, but I decided in the end for David to buy a book of poems by Robert Louis Stephenson, *A Child's Garden of Verses*. They're absolutely magical, and we all enjoy cuddling up of an evening to hear those reassuringly rhythmical verses, in which you can almost imagine yourself back in Keighley, with the trains going past.

For the two oldest boys, I bought a book each that they can later swap. For Adam, I got *The Adventures of Huckleberry Finn* by Mark

Twain, because I never want him to forget how to play. And for Henry, *The Adventures of Tom Sawyer*. I know we'll have such fun reading those together. I think I'll suggest we each read a chapter a night out loud, after the two youngest are in bed.

Being a mother on your own with children isn't always bad. I make the rules, and I have all the joy as well as all the hard work and heartache. Every Christmas I remember all the people I've lost, beginning with you, Mama. After losing you, things were fairly stable though, until within the space of just one year I lost my English parents, my darling little Stephen, my rock Stan, and Uncle Harold. And most recently, of course, I lost the best friend I probably ever had, Hilda. Now that I've lived in more than one place in England, I also miss people who are still alive but hundreds of miles away, including Cath and Millie, and Auntie Margaret. I wonder if it ever gets any easier, missing people? At times, I wonder how I can keep going. I have this bottomless pit in my chest that seems to suck inwards and downwards, draining every ounce of energy into it. But I keep putting one foot in front of another, cleaning, and cooking, and washing, and ironing (what I have to), and polishing, and washing up. Thank God for my writing, Mama, which gives me hope. Although I'm writing about being a war widow, I try to make it funny, focussing on the little things the children do that make me laugh—like when this week, David looked at my flabby arms (they're not nearly as firm as they were when I was in Yorkshire) and frowned as he kneaded them, pulling the skin this way and that. I watched and waited for whatever was in his little head to come out, then he spoke, still frowning:

"I wish I had skin like yours, Mummy. Yours is nice and loose, and I think mine's too tight for me. Look!"

He held up his chubby little arm with its lovely smooth, tight skin to show me how unfortunate he was, compared to me. I just pulled him to me and hugged him so that he couldn't see me smile, and I told him not to worry, one day he would have skin like mine—but in the meantime, it will grow with him.

5th January 1942

Shirley has had the most beautiful little girl! I went round to see her this morning, taking a few things belonging to Susan that I hope will come in handy. Susan's so big now. She's almost ten months old, Mama—you would hardly believe how she's grown.

Shirley's having trouble feeding, this time. She confided that she's very sore, and her right bosom is hot to the touch. She didn't look well. I told her to tell the midwife, who was due to pop in this afternoon. She'll hopefully sort her out, but I suggested a warm flannel on it in the meantime.

12th January 1942

Poor, dear Sandhya. She's just found out that her lovely husband is now a POW. She is, unsurprisingly, beside herself with worry. She seems to suffer from her nerves at the best of times, and this isn't helping.

It seems this war brings a lot of things to be worried about. But there's an old saying, isn't there? Whatever doesn't kill you, makes you stronger. That's a good one to have by you, when times are tough. It's a sort of moral version of having the larder stocked with tins, for when fresh food gets short. I seem to have needed the tinned stuff a fair bit in the last year and a quarter, but now my own predicament isn't quite so urgent I find myself frantically searching for supplies that might ease other people's worries. I'm lucky. I'm alive; I still have most of my children (God rest Stephen's soul); and although I miss Stan each and every day, I will be forever grateful to him that he provided for me by making sure we have a roof over our heads. Plus, I've found something I can do, and love doing. Well, two things really, if you count the gardening as well as my writing. No, I'm a very lucky woman. We should always count our blessings, because it doesn't do to sit there feeling sorry for yourself, does it, Mama? I never saw you doing that.

27th *January 1942*

I've been very busy since Christmas, catching up on my writing. What with losing Hilda, and then Christmas, I've struggled to make my commitment, but I'm now ahead of myself with stories to tell about making do and mending, about friendships between women, about loss of life and new life. Not to mention the recipes. I try to steer away from controversial topics.

The Yanks have decided to send troops over to Britain. Of course, they joined the war back in December, but I suppose they wanted their GIs to have Christmas with their families, before sending them off to fight. You never know whether a man will return, once he's at war. Everyone I speak to, Mama, is very excited about them coming to be stationed on British soil. I'm reserving judgement.

1st *February 1942*

I can't believe Shirley's little girl is a month old, Mama! She came round to see me today, and I made us a spot of lunch. The tea flowed thick and fast, as did the gossip. It turns out she had mastitis when I went to see her. The midwife thankfully eased it for her, but she was quite poorly for a while, I believe. She downplays everything, does Shirley. Not one to complain. But it was nice to catch up with an old friend. Life's been so full of changes, I sometimes feel the need to connect to my girlhood, a bit like feeling down beside the green shoots for a carrot or beet.

8th February 1942

I decided to go to a dance on Saturday, to cheer myself up. Adam said he'd keep a listen out for the young ones. He's a good boy and always does his homework. I don't understand half of what he's doing of course. But I make sure I show an interest. I'm hoping I'll learn along with him. So, I happily test him on his French spellings and English grammar. It's the French pronunciation I'm not so good at. I can keep up with the mathematics so far, and the English is—not wishing to sound immodest, Mama—easy. One day, I would love to go to one of those universities and learn English really well. Fancy being a university student, able to just read all day long. It's a pipe dream, of course. I read his books when he's not reading them, and then we have a discussion over the dinner table about what I've read. Needless to say, the other two boys tell us to shut up because we're being boring, but I don't care. I'm all fired up. I want to learn everything I can. I've got a lot of catching up to do.

But I've been thinking about what Hilda said, about how we're all equal in the eyes of God, and I don't want to get too big for my boots, Mama. This—well, of course, not London originally, Mama, but London from the age of four—is where I came from. Even before that, I never lived a life of privilege, though I know you always did your best for me—even when you made the decision not to hold onto me, as that man and lady were taking me away from you. I understand now that you had no choice.

I've always had to work for what I have, just like everyone else round here. Wherever I go throughout the rest of my life, and no matter how well my children do, I hope I never forget that. The fact that I have a column in the Telegraph and Argus and some people know my name who have never met me, that doesn't mean I'm better than Iris down the road who takes in washing to make ends meet, does it? She's a good, dear soul who would do anything for anybody. I told Adam:

"Now then, Adam, (sounding right Yorkshire!) you know I want you to do well at school."

He nodded, looking all serious. I could see he was worried about what might be coming next.

"But above all, I want you to enjoy it."

His little face brightened up, like a kid who's just been given a penny.

"And what I want you to learn most can't be found in books," I said. "And that is how to be a man. What Ruth and Nathan would call a *mensch*. Do you know what that means, Adam?"

He shook his head, looking bewildered.

"It's a Yiddish word, Adam. Yiddish is the language a lot of Jewish people use to communicate with each other. Mensch just means human being, but it has a higher meaning, too—a person of integrity and honour. Do you know what integrity means, Adam?"

"Well, I think I do," he said, hesitating.

No definition was forthcoming from him, but of course I've spent many months looking up definitions of words in Uncle Harold's dictionary.

"It's alright. This isn't a school test." I ruffled his hair, and we both chuckled.

"Integrity is the quality of people who have honour, are trustworthy and honest, and fair and decent. People who have what's called a strong moral compass, Adam. People who know instinctively what is right and wrong and which direction to take in life based on that. Wherever you go in life, never forget to pack your moral compass,

Adam. Be kind to people. Don't trample on them. And always be good to any woman you end up with. Then, my son, you will make me very proud."

I finished my little speech by giving him a big hug and pretending to plant wet kisses on his cheeks. When I was done, he looked at me with those lovely big blue eyes of his. A wide smile crept across his face. Then he leaned into me again, wrapping his arms around me, and said:

"You're the bestist Mum in the whole wide world. I love you a million trillion!"

"And I love you too, my darling. I love all my babies," I said, my voice sounding just a teeny bit hoarse.

Later when I asked him about going out to the dance he said:

"You go! It'll do you good, Mum."

10th February 1942

Sandhya came round for a cup of tea today, Mama. It's been a while since we managed to chat properly. She hasn't heard from her hubby, whose Christian name incidentally is Anton. The poor girl has had precious few letters from him. After he was captured, it seems they were marched here, there, and everywhere. She's had two photographs in that time, with sparse details, but the first photo had twenty of them in it, and the second only eight. On the back was written a number, "7188" and "Stalag XXID." She says she prays to God each night to look after her husband, but she's losing faith, which for her is a very big thing indeed. Her priest is worse than useless, it seems. If you ask me, he spends most of his time drinking the communion wine and smoking woodbines. He seems to have very little interest in his congregation, and even less in anyone that isn't from Ireland and knows his family. I think he wants to keep an eye on those ones, in case they tell his mum what he's up to, to be honest. A young chap. This might even be his first parish. I've been along with Sandhya to keep her company once or twice, and he seems to me to be what Ruth would call a shyster. How he got to be a priest, God alone knows. Plus, I didn't like the way he told me he thought I had three lovely boys and offered to give them individual bible study lessons. He can keep his hands off my sons. I wouldn't trust him as far as I can throw him.

Anyway, the long and the short of it is, Sandhya met a GI in the post office the other day. He was buying a postcard of Woolwich to keep for his Mum, when they got chatting. It seems they pay no attention to the fact that you're wearing a wedding ring, these Yanks. They figure they can buy any girl for the price of a pair of nylons. But this particular GI spoke softly and wasn't as brash as some. He told her all about his folks back home in a place called Mantua, which is pronounced Mancha, and is in the state of New Jersey. Over there, the boys don't move far away from their mums. His mum is Italian, so there's a strong sense of family. And of course he's a good Catholic boy. Except, not so good if you ask me. Anyway, they got talking and one thing led to another and before you can say Jack Robinson they're walking together in Shrewsbury Park. Sandhya had an arranged marriage, and she's always tried to be a good wife. The reason their marriages are arranged, she explained to me a while back, is so they find someone who's a good match for them; Indian, Catholic, well educated, and so on. It makes sense, really. Only trouble is, they get to meet each other once, make a decision, and then the two families meet with a big engagement party. The deal is settled before they get a chance to know each other properly. They then have a few more meetings before the wedding, but of course she's expected to serve him as her lord and master. Not that Sandhya's husband isn't kind. She says she's grateful not to be beaten. Talking of which, Mama, there are plenty of girls round here that no longer seem to be bumping into door frames every five minutes, now that their blokes are away in the war. I don't know what I'd have done if my Stan had been that kind. I've seen those women grow taller since their men were called up. They've metamorphosed from little snips of things that were even more mouse-like than I was, to strong, capable and fearless women, able to cope with pretty well anything.

Anyway, it seems all Sandhya and this GI did was hold hands briefly, but Sandhya is convinced she's in love. And so, she's in turmoil. Her husband languishes in some POW camp somewhere far away, desperately clinging to his photograph of her no doubt, while she's realising what else there is out there. Of course, I told her about Lincoln—that's the name of the chap I was dancing with on Saturday— not that there's much to tell.

25th February 1942

I have now entertained Lincoln at my house on three separate occasions. Each time, he's been politeness itself, and each time I could smell the carbolic soap on him as he crossed my threshold. The children pulled back when they saw his face leaning down towards them, even though he was holding out sweeties (candy as he calls it). Of course, the oldest two remembered their manners and said thank you and how d'you do, but David hid behind me, and so Adam had to take his sweets for him and give them to him.

Despite that rather strained introduction, the next time they saw him it was as if he'd never been a stranger. Children don't stand on ceremony or stay wary for long, do they? Adam wanted to know all about where Lincoln's from. He lives in New York, which of course sounds very exciting, but Lincoln tells me the negroes have to live near each other for safety, and if he was caught with a white woman over there he would be lynched. I didn't quite know what lynching meant, but he explained it to me as delicately as he could. It's not pretty, Mama, is all I'll say. He has to be careful over here because his superior officers are white, and there are plenty of white GIs like the ones that made those embarrassing comments to me, who would gladly "tan [his] backside," as he put it.

We didn't spend all our time talking about how awful it is, though. We put on the radio and danced to the music, much to the children's embarrassed delight. He taught me a new and exciting dance called the Jitterbug. It's hard work because it's all on your toes, very fast and energetic. Lincoln throws me about, so it's like being a kid again, tossed around by my dad. You'd think I weighed nothing, the way he lifts me up.

After we'd collapsed into the two armchairs, we sat and told stories about childhood pranks and laughed until our sides hurt. I told him about how David, my brother, used to play knock down ginger with his friends. They'd go along the street and tie a bit of string between several door knockers, then stand on the end and pull. Once the ladies came out of their doors, they'd run away. Lincoln and his chums used to climb up fire escapes in tenement buildings then slide down them, much to the dismay of the old ladies who would come out waving their brooms, threatening to tell their mamas. It's a wonder no one got hurt, because we're talking several floors up.

It feels good to have a laugh, Mama. I'd forgotten what that was like. Lincoln's face spreads into a smile at the slightest provocation and he has a cheeky, little-boy laugh that's so endearing. He laughs with a "he-he-he", like Santa Claus, and his chest kind of caves in as if he's being tickled. Watching him brings a whole new meaning to the expression "tickled pink," though when he blushes it's not quite the same as watching someone of my complexion tell embarrassing tales of days gone by.

26ᵗʰ *February 1942*

Lincoln has asked me if I'll go with him to the dance on Saturday night at the Links, Mama. That's the day after tomorrow! I feel nervous, because I know he's going to want to do the jitterbug with me. We tried out some lifts today in my living room, and he told me I'm a natural. I never knew dancing could be so much fun!

27ᵗʰ *February 1942*

Lincoln told me today, after another dance practice, that he had to take a letter from his commanding officer to a café where he wished to purchase some lunch. The letter asked the owner if he would mind serving him, to which the owner chuckled when he read it. Lincoln told me he started to get nervous and sweat profusely, expecting a scene as might occur back home. But instead, the man came round from behind his counter and slapped him on the back, laughing. He said in a voice loud enough that everyone in there could hear:

"If any of these old codgers dares to object to you eating here, I will have no hesitation in throwing each and every last one of them out on their ears. Half of them are eating on tick, anyhow!"

The other customers glanced at the two of them, a mild look of concern on their faces, then went back to slurping their soup, or tea.

As Lincoln told me this story, his eyes filled up. He shook his bowed head, cradling his cup of tea in his hands.

"How can that man be so nice? I tell you, after what we have to endure with God's help back home, it is a true spark of light. Yessir."

That made me even more determined to dance the jitterbug with him tomorrow.

28th February 1942

Well, I wasn't able to dance with Lincoln. David has chickenpox. Adam and Henry have already had it, but Susan hasn't, of course, so she'll be next. I do hope I haven't missed my chance to dance, Mama.

2nd March 1942

Mama, I was walking across the common today, pushing Susan in her pram. It seemed a nice day for a walk, and it's much easier to push the pram there than up the hill to the park, so I decided to go over to where the Brown School is, and maybe on towards Winns Common.

I'd just bumped into Shirley with her own pram, but she couldn't stop. She had to run an errand for the elderly neighbour she looks after.

As I crossed the road from the Links to the common, there was a woman standing at the bus stop, fagging it and shouting at her kid, telling him to stop crying or she'd give him something to cry about. As soon as she saw me, she stopped mid-scream and turned her head, following me with her eyes.

"Yankee bag!" She whispered as I passed. Then, to my back, "N_ lover!"

Well, actually, she said the whole, despicable word, but I won't stoop so low. I walked on, my back as erect and straight as I could possibly make it, but my eyes stung, and by the time I was safely out of earshot my cheeks were wet, little drips hitting the top of my collar and itching me. I wished I had a cloak to draw round my face so that no one could see me, but I knew I must be strong. I was not about to give in to ignorance, and besides, I know she's in the minority. There seem to be more people behaving like Lincoln's café owner, and I can see by the look in their eyes that many unmarried women envy me.

10th March 1942

In my most recent column for the paper, Mama, I happened to mention the negro GIs, and how badly they get treated by the white soldiers, including their superiors, but Sheila said I can't say that because it might inflame the relationship we have with our American allies. So, I had to tone it down. I wanted also to mention how much more polite they are to our women than the white GIs, but I know that would have been a no-no too, so I merely pointed out what gentlemen the negroes tend to be and let people draw their own conclusions. Anyway, the editor now wants me to do a special feature on them, and she's arranging for a photographer to work with me. I've asked Lincoln if I can interview him and a couple of his pals, and guess what? They all said yes!

15ᵗʰ March 1942

Susan did indeed go down with the chickenpox, Mama, and of course she had it on her very first birthday, but since I still feed her a bit myself, it wasn't too serious. She's over the worst. I made her a cake yesterday for her birthday, which of course was wolfed down by the resident army of boys. She also enjoyed the brown paper in which I'd wrapped her new nightdress, far more than the nightdress itself, haha! I bet I was the same when I was her age, eh, Mama?

This afternoon, Lincoln came to call. The light was particularly good in the living room. I used to entertain him in the front room, but now we know each other better he comes into our living room and makes himself at home. I sat there looking at him as he turned Adam's homework over in his hand. Lincoln's fascinated to read the French words, and he asks me how to pronounce them. I'm not sure I'm getting them right, but I tell him what I know. He's so eager to learn! His absorption gave me a perfect opportunity to study his face, and I thought maybe it's time I took up a pencil again. I haven't drawn anything since before I got married. Henry's a wonderful artist. He brought a lovely charcoal and chalk drawing home the other day, of some apples in a fruit bowl. He'd captured the direction from which the light was coming so beautifully I felt as if I could reach out and eat one. I doubt I can be as good but seeing how well he's doing reminded me how I used to love drawing.

So, I picked up my pencil and some paper and began to sketch. I only had a bit of old scrap paper—a rather distasteful Nazi propaganda leaflet that had been dropped in the street and was otherwise headed straight for the bin—but I decided it would have to do. I studied his broad nose that makes me want to take the flesh into my mouth, his lashes that sit on his cheeks and flutter like little fairies, his high cheekbones with skin stretching over his plump flesh in that way babies' skin does. I tried to capture the shine of his skin, remembering how Henry had used the direction from which the light came. I gave an impression of his tight curls and his collar. I wasn't about to go making a fool of myself by drawing anything below the shoulders. Besides, that would have made me a bit hot under my own collar.

After I'd finished, he looked up, and I realised he'd been keeping still for me, without being told to. He asked so politely, could he see it? I handed it over, but my hand was shaking. What if he thought the picture insulting?

Much to my relief, he looked at it almost tenderly, stroking the edges of his image and shaking his head, mumbling as if to himself:

"Mammy would be so proud of you, soldier."

That was when I made my mind up about something. It involves a letter and waiting for the right time which is never my strong point.

16th March 1942

Today, I saw Lincoln on his way to post a letter, so I asked to see his handwriting. I said you can tell a lot about a man from his handwriting, which is true. I added that I wondered if American men's writing was different from British men's. I was shocked to see he had printed everything, as if he was still in the infants' school. But then I realised, he probably hasn't had much schooling. Over there, coloured people don't have the same opportunities as white people. I know for a fact that while they're here the coloured soldiers aren't allowed to bear arms. Their jobs are all in maintenance and engineering and such like.

"Oh, your writing's lovely!" I lied." Is this to your mama?"

"Yes 'm. Yes, it is." His face was solemn.

I committed his address to memory, silently rehearsing it all the way home after I hurriedly handed the letter back to him, making the excuse that I had to cook.

17th *March 1942*

Last night, I went on one of my travels, this time to a country I've never visited.

I'm in a neighbourhood where all the people look like Lincoln, and it dawns on me that I know why I've come here.

I find her at a sink, a single light bulb hanging from the ceiling with no lampshade as she scrubs away at a shirt collar. Her knobbly knuckles stick out at all sorts of angles. She winces, stands herself up straight, and blinks, her eyes squinting out of deep, dark caverns. I want to reach out and put my arm round her, but instead I hover behind her. I speak gently, afraid of scaring her:

"I know your boy, Lincoln, Mrs Crawford. He's a good man. You must be very proud of him."

At first, I'm not sure she can hear me, but then she stops what she's doing. She never turns her head or replies. I just know she's heard, somewhere deep inside herself.

I wanted to say more, but my visit was brief. All too soon I found myself awake, at home in my bed.

I've since written down the words I wanted to say on writing paper, placed the paper in an envelope, and gone to the post office with it:

Dear Mrs. Crawford,

I hope you won't mind me writing to you. I am a war widow, and in the short time we have known each other, Lincoln has become a good friend to both me and my children.

When I first met him, I was surprised by how different he was from the other GIs. Your son is a perfect gentleman. He always holds the door open for me, and until we had known each other long enough for him to treat me with some familiarity, he always called me Ma'am. I want you to know he has never treated me with anything but the utmost respect.

He is also a very brave soldier.

I am sure you are already very proud of him, but I just want you to know that you are rightly so.

Yours sincerely,

Agnes Cockroft (Mrs.)

I do hope she's pleased to receive that, Mama. Oh, and I included the drawing I did of Lincoln.

18th *March 1942*

I interviewed Lincoln and his pals today, Mama. It felt strange, asking formal questions of him, but he was a good sport and answered everything I asked. I've found out where they all come from, what they were doing before the war, who has a sweetheart back home, and what they tell—and don't tell—their mothers. I also had to ask what they love about England, and I asked them what they dislike too, but they were all too polite to admit to anything. Anyway, I have some nice juicy quotes for the sub-editor to choose from for the headline, and I'll type my story tomorrow.

20ᵗʰ March 1942

Our Henry is eleven years old, and in September he will change schools!

I made a bit of a fuss of him today. Lincoln came round with a fancy cake and a toy car. God knows where he got them from, but he wouldn't take any money. Henry's face was a picture.

After the celebrations, I asked Lincoln to sit down in one of the armchairs, as I had a big favour to ask of him.

"Anything, Frances. You know I would do anything for you."

He looked up at me with that wide open innocence that makes me feel a stirring down below, and a swelling in my chest, both of which I pushed firmly down.

"Lincoln, my little girl will be christened next month. Actually, it's very soon—April 11."

"Why, that's wonderful, Frances!"

"Yes. Yes, it is. Um—Lincoln, I would like to ask you to be Susan's godfather."

I fiddled with my apron. Lincoln stared at me, not breathing. I could see his smile disappear, and for a moment, I was certain I'd offended him. He looked down at his hands for an agonizing few seconds. I wished I could see his face so that I might know what was going through his mind. When he looked up again, his eyes were wet.

"That truly is the greatest honour you could have done me, Frances—" He pushed his spectacles closer to the bridge of his nose. "—apart, that is, from the greatest honour of all, which sadly I can never ask of you."

I got up out of my chair feeling about a stone lighter, and I knelt down beside him. I took his lovely, strong dark hands in mine. Hands I have held on the dance floor but never off it before.

"Thank you, my friend."

"Just one more thing." A cloud crept across his face. "I will have to ask my C.O."

22ⁿᵈ *March 1942*

Saturday night last night! Oh, my God, what a night! The very best, and the very worst, all rolled into one.

Lincoln came for me at seven o'clock sharp, looking as handsome as ever and smelling just as sweet. He held my hand as we entered the hall, his face beaming from ear to ear. First, he led me to a table and bade me put my things down, then he immediately whisked me onto the floor for a quickstep. I could feel all eyes on us as he almost carried me across the floor. I felt as light as air.

Next came a waltz. It just felt right to lie my head on his shoulder this time. We've become so close; the usual distance of a waltz didn't seem necessary. And then another waltz. And another, and I wished they could last forever.

Then the lindy hop music started; the music the BBC considers just a bit too dangerous for them to play, which of course makes everyone want to hear it. Oh, my God, the crowd went wild! One couple got up, and when I saw how good they were, I was glad Lincoln had taught me some moves. We had practised him throwing me up in the air, and I'd learned to land as well as I could and just keep on dancing, but when we executed that particular move, my skirt went flying up at the back to cat calls from the white GIs lurking, as ever, in the doorway.

And then it started. One of the white soldiers broke all the rules of segregation and tried to do an excuse me, pushing and shoving at Lincoln's shoulders. I tried to hold onto my dance partner, but before long there were three of them all shoving at him, and I lost my grip, just like I did as a little girl from you, Mama. A fourth man tried to grab my hands for a dance, but I pushed him off and told him in no uncertain terms I did not wish to dance with him now, nor at any point in the future. He looked shocked, as if he's not used to hearing that from a woman. He tried buying me off with a pair of nylon stockings and some fags, but I stood as tall as my stature would allow and told him I'm fine painting lines on my bare legs thank you very much. As it happens, I have developed a liking for the cigarettes, and under any other circumstances, I would have jumped at the offer, but I wasn't about to tell him that.

I could just about see that, at the far end of the room, Lincoln was down on the floor and three or four boys—because they were just boys, no more than about sixteen or seventeen—were kicking him. My heart raced, and my brain went foggy as my legs ran without me telling them to.

I found myself standing right behind them. They were like a bunch of wolves who'd caught the scent of their prey, and nothing was going to stop them. A couple of girls were crying and squeaking at them, saying things like:

"That's enough now, Charlie!" and "He don't deserve that."

But the mob were deaf to it all.

Out of somewhere came a booming voice, deep and loud enough to wake the dead.

"Stop it NOW! Get off him before I call the M.P.!"

And then I realised the boom had come from deep inside my own body. That was *my* voice. They stopped what they were doing and looked around to see where the sound had come from. I wasn't done, though.

"I've got a son not much younger than you little thugs! I've a good mind to knock your heads together! Is this how your mothers brought you up? To beat up a fellow soldier who's ready to die for your sorry backsides? Now help him up, clean him up, say sorry, and I don't ever want to see you behaving like this again, or you won't be welcome round here, I can tell you!"

I wasn't entirely sure about that last bit, but it seems I was right as the whole assembled representation of British womanhood appeared behind me, shouting in the idiom they would understand:

"Damn right!"

The hoodlums looked like animals in the abattoir, stunned before slaughter. They looked at one another, jaws dropping and eyes wide, then without discussing it they reached down to Lincoln who was by now sitting up, holding his side. From the look of him, I thought he might have some cracked ribs, so I told them they had better get him to see the company doctor pronto. And just for good measure, I told them I would be checking up on them. Of course, I haven't got a clue how I would do that, but I suspect that by then the threat was enough.

Lincoln looked up at me, a smile in his eyes that he dared not show on his lips or cheeks. A smile that seemed to say he was proud of me. Of course I might have imagined it, but somehow, I don't think so. It's the first time I can remember ever seeing a man proud of a woman for sounding strong and standing up for what she believed to be right. He nodded almost imperceptibly to me as he stood up, wincing.

After it was all over and Lincoln had reassured me he'd be OK going off with the white GIs (each one with their hands in their pockets and heads bowed), I realised my knees were about to give out on me. Someone found me a chair, and someone else brought me a half pint of shandy and a cigarette. I drank the shandy down nearly in one, but the cigarette made me cough, so I gave it to someone else.

I went home and looked at myself in the mirror, then said to the grown woman I saw there:

"Well, you wouldn't have done that a couple of years ago, would you? There's no stopping you now, lady!"

That bloody C.O., pardon my language, Mama, had better not refuse Lincoln the time to attend his goddaughter's christening, or there will now be hell to pay.

27th *March 1942*

I went to a different butcher's shop today to buy the meat for the weekend because my usual one was away on family business. When I walked in, the gaffer started talking to his boy in back slang:

"Eh, yob! Evatch a kool! Totch!"

"Say. The elrig I reatch evol's that reggin." Said as the butcher's boy casually chopped into a side of beef.

I calmed the swell inside me, ensuring I looked as cool and in command as Ingrid Bergman.

"My husband was a butcher. Perhaps you knew him? Stanley Cockroft." I waited for the penny to drop. The boy stopped chopping, and the butcher stamped on his cigarette, grinding it into the bloodied sawdust.

"He taught me quite a lot of back slang, actually. I'll take it as a compliment that you think I'm hot."

I clutched my handbag in front of me, my shopping bag on the floor beside me.

"But I won't buy meat from anyone who gossips about my good friend Lincoln, or calls him horrid names, thank you. Next time, you might want to watch your language."

And with that, I turned on my heels. There will be no fresh meat this weekend. I shall have to make do with tinned. I'll make a steak and kidney pudding. The children might miss their roast, but they love a good steak and kidney pud.

11th April 1942

Today was Susan's christening, Mama. A sad and proud day. I watched as Lincoln held Susan in his arms, his brown-black skin making her own look like my sheets on washday after I've used dolly blue on them. The gown was worn by each of her brothers before her, the last time being my darling Stephen. Seeing her in that lovely long dress brought it all flooding back—all the losses I've faced since this bloody war started, and since just before the last war when I lost you, Mama. I had to hold onto Shirley. She knew, bless her, without me having to explain. That's what good friends are all about, aren't they? Not having to use words. Not having to explain yourself. Knowing each other, inside out. It was good to have my brother David there too, and Brenda, who of course was Susan's other godmother. If David was affronted that I chose Lincoln as godfather he never showed it, though I could see him looking out the corner of his eye at us together. I know what he was thinking, but I don't care. Let him think it. It's my life, and I can do with it what I want. In any case, he's wrong. Lincoln is a true, dear friend, but we can never be more than that to each other. The distances we would have to cross are too great—too beset with wolves, and large, unseen, cavernous drops. Neither of us wants to go there. One day, he'll find a nice coloured girl and settle down, and they'll have lovely children together. That lady will be very, very lucky to have such a good, strong, God-fearing and gentle man at her side. I will miss him when he has to leave, as leave I know he must.

When it came to Lincoln's turn to make his oath to help guide Susan in the Christian faith, his voice was so beautifully clear the whole congregation could hear him. My heart swelled to know this man is now part of my family. The link can never be broken, even though we may not see each other. We will write. I hope to God he survives whatever they have in store for him.

Everyone came back to our house afterwards. Both Brenda and Shirley helped hand round sandwiches and cake, specially made by yours truly. I asked David to get a few beers in for the men, and we women had lemonade. Brenda had a bit of beer in hers to make a shandy, but I wasn't bothered. Lincoln stood up, and I couldn't help thinking about how he learned to behave around white people, letting them have seats in preference to himself—whereas when we're alone together, he quite happily sits in those very same armchairs.

12th May 1942

I've decided to make this my last diary entry, Mama. As you can see, I haven't written in it for a while. So much has changed that I no longer feel the need for it. I'm writing this in my garden, with the scent of honeysuckle in my nostrils. The vegetables are coming on. There are rows of runner beans and peas up against the wall, as well as tomato plants. The potatoes are hidden in the earth in the allotment, and the carrots are doing well there too, as are the cabbages. I keep flowers around the edges here in the garden, because beauty is as important as sustenance.

Lincoln's battalion has moved on to fight somewhere, I know not where. He's promised to write, and I will reciprocate. So long as we are both alive, I know I won't lose touch with him. I hope Susan will get to know her godfather, in time. Who knows? In all the time he was here, he never even kissed me, though on one occasion when I was stroking his hands, he told me to stop, or he would not be able to be responsible for his actions. I had wondered if he liked women, but then if I'm honest, I always knew he would have liked more from his relationship with me. It was just too dangerous for him, and too big a jump for me. Maybe one day we will meet again. Whether we do or not, I'm grateful for the time we had together.

Susan is sleeping in her pram, and the wood pigeons are doing their usual thing of sounding like they're just getting going with a bit of gossip when something stops them mid-sentence. It's a warm day, so I decided to afford myself this little luxury of sitting here and writing one last diary entry to you, Mama. I don't know if you will ever read it, but thank you for being there, watching and listening as I recorded the vicissitudes of war and my own insignificant story within them. I had no idea when I started my diary, just how much I would change over the time I've been writing. I was happy with my life, being Stan's wife and a good mother, or so I thought. But the desire some men have for power intervened, and the story I'd written for myself in which we lived happily ever after was irrevocably and cruelly changed through an evil war that robs mothers of sons, young women of their husbands and lovers, and many people of all colours and religions of their loved ones and friends. Despite all, in the midst of all that evil, I met a woman who changed my life. A quiet and unassuming woman who taught me that I am as good as anyone. No better, just as good. No one is any better because we are all human beings who need love, food, and protection just as much as the next person. And in time, we will all die. No amount of money or power can buy you eternal life.

Of course, it's not just women who've helped me. There's Uncle Harold, for starters. But if it hadn't been for Hilda in particular, I doubt I would have found the strength to fight first for Stan, and later for my very dear friend Lincoln. Lincoln and I share one very important thing; we know what it is to be different. I now understand why some Jewish people have pretended through the years that they were something other than Jewish, sad though it makes me to know they felt forced to do so. They were probably wise, to save their necks. That's what I did, too. Instinctively, I knew this country wasn't ready for a brown-skinned girl, so I pretended my complexion was inherited from some exotic Celtic wing of the family. It wasn't hard to do with white adoptive parents. After all, my biological father was probably white. Who knows? He might well have been of Scottish origin, as so many were in South Island. I convinced myself I was telling the truth. But I left out important details. I hope you won't think me cowardly, Mama. Knowing Lincoln has made me even more wary.

Which leads me on to tell you what I plan to do, Mama. I'm going to tell the world my story, though I might change my name. I hope one day the world will be a different place—a place in which everyone knows what Hilda held in her heart. Then, I will be able to proudly announce who I am, and stand shoulder to shoulder with people everywhere, no matter what their colour or religion, whether they are brainy or a bit slow, whether they are the best runner on God's earth or need help to walk, and whether, like Cath and Millie, they love people of the same sex, or like me, the opposite.

I'm going indoors now. It's time to make the children's tea. This is the last thing I will write. I love you, Mama. I will call your name on the wind with sadness and pride, until the day I die.

Your daughter,

Ahurewa.

ACKNOWLEDGMENTS

I would be a far poorer writer without my critical friends. This includes the members of Mossley Writers, led by the indefatigable Sophie Parkes-Neild, herself an inspirational writer and best-selling author. I must extend my thanks to the Oldham National Novel Writing group, led in Oldham by Jacqueline Ward at Oldham Library, and to the staff of Oldham Library, where I penned the first words of this novel in November 2018. Jacqueline has been my cheerleader when I might have given up.

I am grateful to those people who kindly read an earlier version of this novel and gave detailed feedback that enabled me to hone the story, and how I tell it: Gillian Barry; Katie Brumpton; Irene Double; Stephen Moon; and Caroline Wright.

My late mother and father each told me wartime stories, many of which have become woven into this novel, especially Mum's experiences of both the Blitz and evacuation. It was from Dad that I learned, among other useful things, the back slang for "have a look." However, I have not just relied on oral history. I delved into too many online resources to mention here, but I am indebted to the wonderful BBC archive of personal wartime stories, and I am grateful to Barry Attoe, Discovery Room Manager at the Post Office Museum, for information on the London delivery service during World War Two.

As always, I don't know where I would be without my most honest critic and greatest supporter, my husband Philip Spence, who never complains about me spending long hours with my other lover, my computer, when he would far rather have me tramping with him up some hill, somewhere.

Between the Lines Publishing first published Bonnie's debut novel, *A Kind of Family*, in January 2020, when it received 5-star reviews on Amazon and Goodreads. It was later re-released in 2024 and reached #2 in the Amazon charts for step-parents and children. In 2021, Bonnie self-published a joint memoir with her sister and Between the Lines author Jackie Hales.

Several literary journals and anthologies, including MsLexia, Ellipsis Zine, Tiny Molecules, MsLexia, Roi Fainéant, Ad Hoc Fiction, Reflex Press, The Dribble Drabble Review, and Briefly Zine, have published Bonnie's shorter writings. Her work has been listed for the Reflex Press flash fiction competition and shortlisted out of more than 3,000 entries for the King Lear Chairman's Prize. Her nominations include "Best small fictions" and "Best of the net."

Bonnie lives in Greater Manchester, UK, where she shares a house with her husband, various offspring that she is never entirely confident have finally left, and from time-to-time grandchildren, whose size is inconsistent with their conviction that they rule the roost. To relax, she grows vegetables that misbehave even more than the grandchildren, walks in the hills, reads, and dances. She also travels alarming distances now and then, to visit people she loves who have inconveniently chosen to live as far away from her as possible, in Aotearoa/New Zealand. She blogs about becoming an older woman in the UK.